LEAVE IF YOU CAN

Leave If You Can

by

Luise Rinser

Translated from the German by

Margaret Stevens

Arx Publishing
Merchantville, NJ

Originally published as:
"Geh fort, wenn Du kannst"
© 1959 S. Fischer Verlag, Frankfurt am Main.
All rights reserved by S. Fischer Verlag GmbH,
Frankfurt am Main

This edition:
Arx Publishing,
Merchantville, NJ

English translation
© 2010 Margaret Stevens
All Rights Reserved

ISBN 978-1-935228-04-2

Library of Congress Cataloging-in-Publication Data

Rinser, Luise, 1911-2002.
  [Geh fort wenn du kannst. English]
  Leave if you can / by Luise Rinser ; translated from the
German by Margaret Stevens.
      p. cm.
  Originally published in German as Geh fort wenn du kannst.
  ISBN 978-1-935228-04-2
  1. World War, 1939-1945--Italy--Fiction. I. Stevens,
Margaret, 1938- II. Title.
  PT2635.I68G4213 2010
  833'.912--dc22
                              2010031615

Introduction

Italy's experience in the Second World War may be summed up in a single word: catastrophic. Prior to the war, under the rule of the fascist dictator Benito Mussolini, Italy was seen as a major military power and an equal partner with Nazi Germany in the Axis alliance. However, Italy's military weakness was revealed as soon as the country entered the war in June 1940. Invading southern France just as the French government fled Paris to escape the German blitz in the north, the Italian army was unable to make significant headway against the dispirited French even under such favorable circumstances.

Following this inauspicious beginning, the Italians suffered one military disaster after another, both on land and at sea. By the summer of 1943, after the Allied invasion of Sicily, the Italian people had had enough. Mussolini was ousted from power and the new Italian government under Marshal Badoglio immediately began negotiating an armistice with the Allies which was signed in secret on September 3, 1943. Five days later, when the surrender was made public, the Germans moved to occupy the country and oppose the Allied advance up the peninsula. There ensued some of the most bitter fighting of World War II. What was supposed to be an easy campaign through "the soft underbelly of the Axis" ended up a murderous crawl for the Allied armies over rough terrain and fortified hilltops.

The goal of the Allied offensive in early 1944 was the liberation of Rome—the Eternal City. To reach it, they would have to breach the Gustav Line: a string of German fortifications, mine-fields, bunkers, and machine-gun nests stretching the breadth of Italy about 70 miles south of Rome. Anchoring this line were the mountains around a small village called Monte Cassino, made famous by the ancient abbey perched high on the hill above it. Originally founded by Saint Benedict of Nursia in the sixth century AD, the abbey, with its thick masonry walls and dominating position, was seen as an obstacle to the Allied advance. To neutralize this perceived threat, the Allied commanders decided to bomb the beautiful abbey to rubble. This action would go down as one of the most controversial and foolhardy military decisions of the Second World War.

At this stage of the war, an Italian resistance movement made up of communists and other anti-fascists began operating against the occupying Germans. Working behind German lines, the partisans conducted sabotage, launched guerilla raids, organized labor strikes, and harassed the German supply lines. By the end of the war, hundreds of thousands of Italians had joined in the fight.

Leave If You Can is set during this tumultuous time. It is the story of two idealistic young women who rush off to join the partisans to fight for what they perceive to be a just cause. However, earthly causes, no matter how seemingly noble, are sometimes usurped by higher callings.

*"Egredere modo, frater,
egredere si potes."*

Saint Scholastica to her brother, Saint Benedict

*"Laqueus contritus est
et nos liberati sumus."*

Psalm 124

The letter begins...

I suppose, Sir, that having waited what must seem like an age for this account to reach you, you will have given up expecting it and added this disappointment to the many you have already had. And now that the story is in your hands at last, it will carry further disappointment and cause you more pain, not least because you are getting it from a stranger rather than your daughter.

But we have met before...and I think you may remember me. Four months ago, when you were sitting in our convent parlor at Maria del Monte, I was the sister who came to ask you to wait just a little longer.

"I know all about waiting," you retorted.

My immediate reaction to your bitter tone was to wish you were my father rather than Angelina's, so that I could rush over and comfort you. And that's the way I still feel. At the time, though, I found not a single word to express this feeling. I just had to go, leaving you alone with your grief — and a fast-fading hope.

And I was the one sent back to the parlor

— *after you and Angelina had been alone together for a long, long time — sent, that is, to end the agony and ask you to wait for Mother Abbess.*

And that meant I was there when you and Angelina said goodbye to each other.

You used very harsh words and made no attempt to understand her. You said that, seeing she insisted on putting her selfish desire for the cloister before a natural and proper love for her own father, you were forced to look upon her decision to stay in the convent as nothing other than a cowardly escape, and view all her piety as insincere and a lie. You went on to say that she clearly preferred 'the so-called good of her soul' to the well-being and good of humanity, and her stubborn refusal to leave the abbey you took to be nothing less than a fundamental misunderstanding of the greatest commandment given by the One she was professing to obey.

That is what you said, and Angelina listened without defending herself. Up to then she had tried, but by the time I arrived, she was exhausted and could only manage to whisper goodbye in a few words meant for you alone. Maybe you did not even hear.

And I was the only one who saw her tears when the door had closed behind us. We cried together as we had done the day we first met, which is where I am going to begin my story.

You see, I am not going to try and explain Angelina's decision. That sort of thing cannot be explained. I trust that by the time you have read my story through you will have realized even the word 'decision' is wrong. The lot falls, and one is chosen. Resistance is out of the question. Anyone who succeeds in resisting is not a genuine 'chosen one'. Our freedom lies in joyfully accepting the choice that is not to be denied.

<hr />

It is now four months since you went away, and your daughter has had no word from you. Silent and hopeless, you have sat waiting for the story you wanted Mother Abbess to ask your daughter to write. Mother did order her to write it, but for the first time ever, Angelina begged to be released from her vow of obedience. When this was refused, she put together such a boring string of figures, dates and place-names that it would have told you nothing. Believe me, you are much better off with my version, because in that way you will learn what Angelina herself would never have let you see – how brave and loyal she was, how bold to the point of recklessness and how totally committed in all she did, whether as partisan*, or as novice and nun.

The first part will make you happy and leave you feeling proud to recognize her as the daughter you once knew. But the second will prove no easy reading. You will have to follow in Angelina's footsteps — down a path which is bound to seem strange and unappealing, foolish and quite beyond your power to comprehend. No one can help you there. That's how it all happened, and despite not understanding you will simply have to accept it, as one must every act of Providence, great or small.

**Partisan:* member of the anti-Fascist/anti-Nazi resistance.

The story begins...

Angelina arrived at our farm towards evening on the 29th of May 1943.

I watched her coming, not from Perugia but down from the north, across the fields and up the mountain; and not by the road, but along the path used only by us at the farm. She made straight for the little door, by now quite overgrown with ivy as it was never used once the kitchen had its new entrance.

She came to a halt in front of the ivy-covered door, clearly bewildered. I called out to her, asking what she wanted. She was looking for Signora Antonucci she said.

Well Signora Antonucci had died a year ago and there were no Antonuccis around now. Both sons were in the Lipari Islands,* their wives and children goodness knows where. The farm had been taken over by the Fascists and given to an official who happened to be my uncle, and he had taken me in as a maid after my father had died in the Islands.

Lipari Islands: where the Italian Fascists interned political prisoners.

I told the strange girl all this and she listened, fixing her eyes on me and not saying a word. And I couldn't help noticing that, when she stared, her skin stretched itself so tight over her cheekbones that there seemed to be no flesh whatsoever between skin and bone. Then she jerked her head aside as if avoiding a blow, and without turning round again, made as if to be off.

I reached out and stopped her — putting my arms around her and bringing us face to face. Somehow her face seemed familiar to me — extremely familiar, in fact. Whose did it remind me of? Given fairer skin and hair I would have called it *vezzoso*. (I'm not sure if your German word *lieblich** is how that translates.) But as it was, the combination of dark hair, brown skin and ever-so-slightly too prominent cheekbones made me think 'gypsy'. Only one family in the neighborhood had faces like that — beautiful, wild, passionate and secretive — the Antonuccis. It was just that the wide-open, grey eyes had seemed not to fit and had prevented me from recognizing her at first. Yes, it was definitely the face of an Antonucci,

---

**Lieblich:* lovely.

and I suddenly realized who had come.

"Angelina," I said. "Don't be afraid. I'm Giulia, and you're no stranger to *me*! You're Signora Antonucci's granddaughter, and your father is German. We used to play with each other when we were very small, and later on we sang together."

We both started crying, and went to my bedroom where we told each other everything and cried again.

That was the first time I saw Angelina cry. In all the years since, I never again saw her really in tears until the door had closed behind you.

The first time our tears were for what we had both gone through. We had both had to abandon our studies — Angelina, medicine, and I, modern languages. Each of us had lost a father and a home...how could anyone have guessed that you were still alive and would come back from Russia after so many years?* We were both Communists, sharing the same wholehearted belief in the Party Ideal and preferring to die rather than abandon it or give up believing it would bring world happiness.

---

back from Russia: Angelina's father may have been a German prisoner of war captured on the Russian front.

But what were we to do now? Angelina had run away from Germany to take refuge with her *nonna**, but 'Nonna' was dead. I wanted to talk her into staying at my uncle's and working on the farm like me, but the suggestion made her wild.

"Work for a Fascist? I'd sooner starve!" she said. And that was her all over. She would not touch so much as a scrap of bread or swallow a drop of wine.

"Come on," she said. "We're leaving."

"But where are we going?"

"The crowds already on the roads don't know where they're going either," she pointed out and added, "We're bound to end up wherever we're supposed to be."

Her quiet conviction forced me to accept without a second thought.

<hr>

We went off secretly that night, taking nothing but a shoulder-bag each with the bare essentials, and the money that Angelina carried in a belt next to her skin. The dog lying

---

nonna: grandmother.

fastened to its chain barked loud and long, but no one came after us. If my uncle saw or heard, he certainly made no attempt to fetch us back, either then or later. I imagine he was glad to be so easily rid of me, the daughter of a man who had been in the Islands.

We had been walking for some time when I suddenly got scared. We were all right in the dark, but what about daylight and the chance of falling into German hands?

I told Angelina but she carried on walking, and all she said was, "If you're afraid, turn back. I'm going on."

So I followed her, and from that moment on did whatever she said, although I am two years older.

Angelina walked as if she had a goal and knew the precise route. Yet neither she nor I had any idea where we wanted to go. We could easily have been taken for two people out for a walk because we had nothing better to do. Any sensible person would have been bound to think us crazy and as good as lost — after all, two young girls on the road in those days were fair game! Yet Angelina had come all on her own from Germany, and nobody had molested her on the way. This had made her confident and daring – over and above the courage and remarkable foresight she has by nature.

But the other thing — I mean not actually knowing where we wanted to get to — that was a real adventure! It was quite spontaneous, like children leaving home in a temper or driven only by some vague longing, with no plan in mind. But actually it was something else entirely. Angelina's boldness appeared to have greatly challenged fate and guaranteed her special protection. I could put it more simply if you were open to it: *she was called and she came.* Where the call would lead she did not then need to know. That would be revealed in due course. And it was, though not until many months later.

At this point you find us still on the road (or the field path, I should say), from Assisi to Foligno.

We were avoiding main roads and broad daylight. Every morning we bought bread and whatever else we needed, then crawled into some hiding-place — an old sheep-pen, somewhere in the bushes or any place we happened across — and slept as best we could.

Once I very nearly parted from Angelina. It was not far from Foligno. We shopped in a *trattoria** kept by an old woman who had lost all three sons. The house was completely run down and she herself sick with grief and work. I told Angelina I wanted to stop there. She said nothing to me. Instead she told the woman we would stay a few days and do what most needed doing. It was the first time I had realized how well and how hard Angelina could work.

"You would have made a good daughter-in-law," the old woman said, and she begged us never to leave.

But one evening a week later, when the house was in order, Angelina said, "I'm going." (Not, "Come on, we're going." Just, "I'm going.")

I've no idea why I went with her, when for the life of me all I wanted was to stop with the old woman and have some measure of safety. The fact is Angelina already had that quality which, fourteen years later, was to make her such an admirable Mistress of Novices: she was never stern or dogmatic, but so clear

---

*trattoria: a casual eatery.

and positive that she was obeyed without question. She always gave the impression she had everything worked out and was simply not saying.

Admittedly, all she wanted right then was just to keep on walking. But what a long road it was from Foligno to Maria del Monte!

<hr/>

On that road I only once saw her disconcerted (or rather twice in one day but for reasons that were linked). I had a 'keepsake' in my pocket; my mother's rosary in a little case. The case fell out and broke open and Angelina saw what was in it.

I was embarrassed. "It's only something to remember my mother by," I said hurriedly.

Angelina gave me a quick glance. "What are you apologizing for?" she asked.

I didn't answer.

"You Italians are all the same," she remarked. "You want world revolution with the Pope as Chief Commissar."

There's some truth in this and I felt ashamed. I dropped the rosary and shuffled it under the dust.

For the next couple of hours neither of us said a word.

This was very early in the day. We were in a very lonely region and felt safe walking right through the morning. I did notice, however, that Angelina was limping. She never complained but in the end it dawned on me she had a large broken blister. Her heel was quite red by that time and I was afraid it might go septic.

When we came to an isolated house with a wall fountain we stopped for a rest, and to let Angelina wash and bandage her foot.

Then the door opened unexpectedly and a voice called out of the semi-darkness, inviting us to come in. Angelina would never have gone in if she hadn't been in such pain.

The house turned out to be a convent, poor and old. And it was a nun who had invited us in. I don't know what order it was; Poor Clares maybe? And I can't remember the name of the convent. It was somewhere not far from Rieti.

We spent the night there. They gave us an empty cell outside the enclosure* and treated

---

enclosure: the part of a convent that only the nuns may enter.

Angelina's foot.

Before I fell asleep, Angelina came over to where I was lying and pressed something into my hand. It was the rosary I had thrown away.

"There you are," she said. "Have it back. You have to stand by what you believe in, whatever it is. I'm no better than you," she added. "Here I am, accepting hospitality from these people — the sort we won't want to tolerate in our new world."

I woke in the night to the sound of singing. They were at prayer in the chapel between midnight and dawn; it was Matins but I did not know it then. I heard it as if in a dream and in the dream I saw Angelina standing at the window, her face in the moonlight showing wet with tears. I didn't dare speak to her.

I thought, she's been crying because she's lonely. But now I know the real reason, and you, Sir, can guess it, too.

Next morning, however, she was more rebellious than usual. The Superior didn't want us to leave; two young girls on the road in wartime…she simply couldn't allow it and she would be more than happy to let us stay.

I am timid by nature and was ready to

agree at once, but not so Angelina.

"What would we do here?" she retorted.

The Superior answered that we could work in the house and garden. Both seemed to me cool and silent and far removed from the war.

But Angelina said, "Millions out there are going hungry, being attacked in their beds, and dying in poverty; and we're supposed to live here in peace and seclusion? So much for 'love thy neighbor'!"

"And you, my dear, intend to dash out and rescue these millions?" The Superior was an old woman and she spoke gently. Angelina turned white but said nothing.

"Very well," said the Superior, "go and do what you believe you must. But remember we too love all people, and tremble more for their fate than for our own. There is more than one way of helping these millions."

"I can't understand that at all," Angelina replied, quietly but firmly. "I'm the daughter of a Communist. I'm a Communist myself. I know only one effective way of helping people. Social need can only be alleviated by social policy on a wide scale. Everything else is escapism and a dream."

I thought this a good answer, the best; the only true answer, in fact.

The Superior simply remarked, "Ah, my child, how short-sighted you are!"

There was nothing more to add so we went. But Angelina had lost her confidence. For two or three days I had to take her place as leader. Then it blew over.

All the same, something new showed in her face from then on, and in the way she spoke. It is hard to describe. I could call it defiance, but I'm not talking about anything sinister. She seemed to be throwing out some kind of challenge.

"Right then, we shall see which of us wins. Whatever happens, I'm sticking to my way."

<hr />

Afterwards we were often asked if we had ever been frightened or threatened by any kind of evil. I must admit there were one or two occasions when I was afraid, but I don't believe Angelina knew the meaning of fear. Once a pack of animals came in sight. I immediately saw wolves and was petrified;

but she maintained they were just stray dogs. I believed her because I wanted to, but I think they *were* in fact wolves from the Abruzzi Range and she knew it. You don't find dogs in packs. Even wild dogs, though, can be dangerous. Whichever they were, they ran away without doing us any harm.

There were other dangers, but as nothing happened to us there is no need to mention them.

We walked on and on and one day found ourselves in a deep, green valley beside a fast-flowing river. The place was totally isolated except for one house, unmistakably an abbey, perched high up on the mountainside above woods of sessile oak. I knew from pictures that it must be Subiaco, and the river the Aniene.

These names didn't mean a thing to Angelina. She knew nothing about Saint Benedict and when I tried to explain all she said was, "Oh don't bother me with *myths*!"

This was history I protested, not myths.

"The things you call history!" she retorted.

"You with your head full of religious gloom! History is as clear as the day. Whatever is not that clear no longer concerns us. I can't see how you ever came to belong to the Party."

There was a good deal I could have said on that subject but I didn't want an argument. Besides, each of us at the same moment heard a sound like someone trying to stifle a sob. Then we caught sight of a young lad of about twelve, hiding under a low wall, crying and beating the ground with his fists. He was too upset and angry to see or hear anything, but Angelina sat down next to him, waited until he had calmed down, and got him to talk.

He had run away from his home in Rieti and was looking for his two older brothers who had gone to the join the partisans in Rome. They hadn't taken him with them because he was too young and ought to be at home with his mamma. But he had felt ashamed and had run away, looking for Rome but not finding it, yet not wanting to go home at any price. He was only a boy but in spite of his tears there was something about him that made us take him seriously.

When Angelina said, "The police will find you

and take you back," he showed us a revolver he had in his pocket and there was no doubt he knew how to use it. Finally we asked him if he knew exactly where his brothers were. Yes, he said, but he was not allowed to tell. Well then, he could keep it to himself and come with us to Rome. That was Angelina's decision.

I was astonished. Not a word had ever been said about going to Rome. For her that would be 'out of the frying-pan into the fire' — Rome was full of Germans.

Though she could pass as an Italian (better than I could, seeing that I'm fair-haired like a German), it was still possible she might be recognized. But she was adamant and we started out again, walking south-west. There were three of us now. The boy's name was Tommaso.

We didn't dare take the Via Tiburtina, nor the Nomentana, nor any of the main roads. But we came at last to Monte Mario, and there — there at our feet — we saw Rome. It was the 26th of June, 1943. None of us three had ever been in Rome before. We stood still for a long while, conscious of nothing but our beating hearts. Then we went down into the city.

In Rome at that time you wouldn't have known there was a war on. We never once saw a German uniform. But there were plenty of men speaking German. These were out of uniform, the plan being to convince the Allies Rome had no military presence, and so ward off any bombardment. The Germans wanted to save the beautiful city of Rome and keep it for themselves.

Angelina maintained they acted out of sentimental attachment to their classical education, and also out of fear that the Vatican might be hit, in which case they would get the blame and no one would ever forgive them. I found it very bewildering watching these Germans going around as if it were peace-time and they were on holiday here. They showed no sign of being involved in the fighting, and posed no threat. They ignored us, but we hated them.

We carried on walking without knowing where we were going. Our tongues were sticking to our gums with thirst and I was completely exhausted; even Angelina was not her usual self.

Then Tommaso suddenly proved he was no longer a child but, like a grown man, had been wise enough to keep quiet until he felt sure he could trust us. He had known all along exactly which part of Rome he was heading for, and now he took us with him. I was anxious, but Angelina said we could risk going with him. Tommaso had an address in Trastevere and we set out to find it.

It turned out to be a *trattoria* — empty at this time of day. There was an old man asleep in a corner. Tommaso woke him and whispered in his ear for some time. The old fellow made no reply but looked us over and, still without saying a word, led us through the back yard into a cellar. There he locked us in! I was really scared, which is hardly surprising, but Angelina and Tommaso kept calm, and that steadied me.

Some time later a young man appeared and questioned us about our command of foreign languages, and whether we were willing to learn to operate wireless sets. He asked us, too, if we were willing to risk sticking with him. From then on we were with the partisans, in the group led by Antonio.

The group was known as *L'Altalena* — 'The Swing'. Antonio called it that because, swing-like, it was now up, now down; sometimes victorious, sometimes in retreat. Its position was unfixed, between earth and sky. He also chose the name because of the exhilaration he used to feel at swinging so high his mother screamed in fright, while he, obsessed with a desire to touch heaven with his feet, tried to go even higher.

This Antonio was an unusual young man, not at all a typical Communist partisan leader. He was slight and almost delicate, a bit like an Arab I thought. His voice was soft and gentle and he used it to issue brief commands. Otherwise he hardly ever spoke, at least not to me. He must have talked more to Angelina because she knew a lot about him. I saw the two of them quite a few times sitting like lovers on the wall at Tevere, not touching, just exchanging looks.

Antonio had been a theology student. Two years before ordination he had suddenly gone over to the Communists. He wanted to study law, but his uncle, a monsignor who had been paying for his studies while he stuck to theology, now wouldn't give him a single lira or help him in any way. No one else would help him either, so he joined the partisans.

Angelina said it was the only path he could take, seeing that his religion couldn't answer the questions plaguing his mind and heart; questions as to why the Church supports private ownership and the rich, why the Holy Father should bless the money-grabbing, power-seeking, hypocritical nations of the West while calling for a fight against Communism which wants a rule of peace on earth. Why does the Church not press for the redistribution of large estates in Italy? And why does God leave the poor in poverty, and teach them patience and submission rather than rebellion against their oppressors? Why preserve the existing state of things, despite its rottenness? Why, why, why?

So Antonio was now a Communist and leader of a group of partisans, and was fighting against the Fascists and the rich, against his religion and against himself; and was not happy doing it. But that was where he stood, and with desperate loyalty he stuck to his post, gaining added strength from Angelina.

For nearly two months we lived like soldiers in barracks, or I should say more like rats in a trap. We lived in the cellar, which smelt of sour wine and was always dingy. We ate and slept there, listening in to foreign broadcasts and secret news coming over the wireless sets.

Angelina had quickly got the hang of decoding these and I translated them into French, English and German for the foreigners who were part of our group. I was often afraid of being caught, which would have led to being shot. Angelina said we were reasonably safe but added that we had no right to take safety or life for granted.

I was almost afraid of her when she spoke like that, although she was not trying to play the heroine and just came straight out with it. This complete lack of compromise in her character was in fact what worried me. I could easily have pictured her as a first-century Christian martyr, and I once told her so. She looked at me somewhat pityingly.

"And down here I suppose you feel like a little heroine for the Faith in the catacombs? I can't see any grounds for that. We're doing our duty and we could be far worse off. Besides, you're forgetting that I should never have been a Christian! My task would have been to incite the people against the emperor."

Then, like the young girls we still were, we spent the next few days making up a long, long story about ourselves revolutionizing first-century Rome.

This was abruptly cut short by news of the plans for Mussolini's downfall, and by the afternoon of the 25th, it had happened.

I thought, the war being over, we would now be let out of our cellar and be free from all danger. But Antonio did something he had never done before and never did again. He stroked my hair, and although he was very little older than me, said in a fatherly tone, "I'm sorry, little one. The *real* war is only just beginning."

They all thought the same — nobody was celebrating. They went around venting their anger in action, destroying all the Fascist signs and slogans they could find; washing them off, breaking them up, striking them out, and tearing them down. The King's words, not the *Duce's**, were now scrawled on the walls of houses. But one could sense that the words had no power to incite. I was disillusioned by it all. Angelina, though, was galvanized.

"Decision time, Giulia," she said. "Things are going to get tougher. If you're afraid," she went on, "you'd better leave. Go home now, while you're still free."

I had no wish to go. I didn't think things would get very bad in the near future, and it turned out that there *was* a quiet time ahead, for *us* at least. But Antonio went off, taking Tommaso with him. The whole group went away into the mountains of Albany. Angelina and I were the only ones to stay behind in our cellar with our sets. A messenger came from Antonio every night to exchange news.

The next few weeks were so exciting I had no time to be afraid. It was the stage when the German parachutists were landing to free Mussolini and bring down the King. The Brennerstrasse† was already having to defend itself, and our Foreign Minister was secretly negotiating a cease-fire with the Allies

---

*That is, Mussolini, nicknamed *Il Duce*—the leader.
†*Brennerstrasse:* Austria-to-Italy supply route.

although the papers did not admit it.

Our group had grown. Five English-speaking South Africans had joined and brought weapons: some twenty-millimeter cannon, three machine-guns — and an extra radio as well.

Our people were busy risking their necks. Some had posts with the Germans and were into espionage and sabotage. One was an aircraft observer, another drove a truck. One of Tommaso's brothers was working as an electrician, listening in to military calls and causing lines to break down so that telegraphed commands came through hours late. And Antonio held all the strands.

This was when we had our first bombing. It was on August 11. Antonio was in Rome and had sent us out for a couple of hours to get some fresh air. We had just got as far as the Piazza Pia when the planes started coming. The Romans were scared. They were screaming and running away from the bombs like sheep from wolves. And where to? We were standing where the Via della Concilazione begins and we saw exactly what happened — they all ran for the Vatican.

I shared their feelings and was ready to join them, but Angelina grabbed hold of me. "Stay here," she said softly, though her face was completely drained of color as it often was when she was extremely angry.

I tried to protest, "Come on. We'll be safe there. Nobody's going to bomb the Vatican!"

"You're wrong," she said. "There can be emergency drops, and some bombs fall too soon, others too late. And there's always the chance of assassins, remember?"

Then she suddenly let go of my arm and shouted, "All right then, run along! Go on, run! Run to your stable where you belong. Oh, you Italians! The Vatican for you is your amulet against the evil eye."

By this time, I was angry too, but I said nothing. All I thought was, "Wouldn't I just love to know, Angelina, how much you'd give right now for any place in the world where you could feel safe and at home!"

Maybe she was thinking the same. "Oh, Giulia," she said, as if in answer, "There's no such thing as security any more, either external or internal."

At that moment something happened, that

for Angelina's sake in particular ought never to have happened, especially seeing it could have been avoided. An old woman had fallen in the crowd. At first people clambered over her as they ran. Then others began to kick her out of the way. Not a soul helped her up. But Angelina fought her way through, helped her onto her feet and led her to one side. While bombs fell in the suburbs we took the old woman home.

⚹⚹❀⚹⚹

I ask you, Sir, how in the world could Angelina or Antonio, or I, or you believe that Christians obey their highest command, to love one another, when we saw them behaving like this? What use was there in pretending we hadn't seen?

⚹⚹❀⚹⚹

Early in September our lives changed. As Angelina had prophesied, things got tough.

With no explanation, and in broad daylight, Antonio had us fetched from Rome in a German military vehicle driven by one of Tommaso's brothers. We were taken to somewhere near

Frosinone, to an area where Antonio had set up a kind of headquarters in the mountains and woods.

Our group was quite large. Most of us were Italians, of course — deserters, anti-Fascists. But besides the South Africans we had Austrians, Germans, some French and an American officer.

I think Antonio was expecting the Allies to land and that was why he had gone into the southwest. But he had miscalculated and some weeks later we headed back into the north. On the Rocca Romana by Lake Bracciano there was a much larger group Antonio wanted to link up with.

But before we left Latium, an event took place that frankly didn't in the least affect the course of the war, but was therefore all the more important for Angelina; and it is your daughter's story I'm telling, don't forget, not the history of the war.

September 9th 1943* was for her a never-to-be-forgotten day, the day when bombs destroyed

---

*On September 3, 1943, the Italians signed an armistice with the Allies at a conference in Sicily. The armistice was kept secret for five days.

Frosinone, (an understandable target with a large, important railway station), but also the day that saw the destruction of one of those tiny towns perched high up in the mountains, towns that from a distance look like fortresses, although as everyone knows they're just a random collection of stone houses of the very poorest kind. It was impossible to think of any reason why this little grey, insignificant town should be destroyed, because it had no military presence. One can only put it down to chance, misjudgment, error. From far off Angelina and I watched everything burn that could burn, and saw the walls collapse. I can still see her standing there motionless, clenched fists pressed against her lips, and eyes fixed unswerving on this unknown, dying town.

Antonio started to urge us on and I called Angelina. But however loudly I called she didn't hear me. I had to shake her to make her come to. That's the only way I can put it. She had to 'regain consciousness' and as she came back to her senses she looked at me, bewildered, as if I were a stranger. She stayed like that all the rest of that day. She spoke only once and then just to ask the name of that little place. Antonio told her and she lapsed back into silence. I was worried about her state of mind. I didn't understand it and she made no attempt to explain.

⚜

I didn't learn what it was all about until long after, and this is something, Sir, you may not want to believe and yet you must, as I now do; you're coming to the part of my story that will show how Angelina sensed her destiny that day.

⚜

It took five months for the course of the war to bring us back to that region; five months for Angelina to come again to that small town which was the unknown goal of all her wanderings. It came about through circumstances not unusual in wartime, but we found it very strange all the same.

⚜

Meanwhile a great deal happened in those five months, a time when Angelina was just as you would wish to find her; every bit your daughter, loyal and fearless as a man, and apparently easy to fathom.

I shall tell you more about that period in a while. For the time being I shall be brief. But I ought to say right away that, looked at in the light of her true life, what Angelina did at that stage had little meaning. Yet those months, in which her courage, loyalty and obedience were severely tested, have to be seen as good training for the cloister.

Angelina found nothing remarkable in all this. For her it was simply a case of doing what had to be done. Yet she amazed the rest of us.

⚜

On October 16th we found ourselves surrounded by the Germans. They had combed through the forests by Lake Bracciano, and we were caught in the net. Angelina and I were in no danger; we were out gathering mushrooms, had no weapons, and were nothing to do with the partisans. Our folk were armed but there was no sense in shooting because the Germans outnumbered them by far. Antonio gave the command to surrender without resistance and they obeyed. They were taken to the next village where they were held in the square, hour after hour, waiting for a decision.

I thought all was lost, but Angelina said I ought to know Antonio and how he always got himself and his people out of any trap.

A while later, a major drove up and went into the headquarters. We could hear a conversation that quickly turned into a quarrel. They were yelling at one another. You couldn't understand a word. The only place to hear anything clearly would have been right outside the window, but the window was on the second floor. Then Angelina did the only thing that could be done. She climbed an oak tree at the back of the house, and from there got onto the roof, where she listened to the conversation — down the chimney! It went on for some time, but by the end Angelina had found out all she needed to know.

The captain was in favor of a shooting, the lieutenant colonel spoke out against this and the major, whom they had called in, handed over the decision-making to someone else. Antonio's people were to be taken to a camp first.

The camp was two hours away. Seeing there were just twenty prisoners — not of vital importance to the course of the war — the Germans thought just four heavily-armed soldiers would be enough to send with them. Angelina managed to convey all this to Antonio as she walked past and we realized that something had to happen on the way to the camp if our men were to be rescued.

Angelina's first try at helping didn't work. She attempted to persuade the young men of the village to follow and overpower the Germans. But no one dared, and when she asked for a weapon they made out they didn't have any.

This to-ing and fro-ing lost us valuable time and our party had already trailed out of sight. Then Angelina began to run, and I with her. I have no idea whether she had a plan, but plan or no plan, she succeeded in what she wanted to do.

The road passed through a ravine. We reached this ravine before them because we took a short-cut along a goat's path to a place where we could look down into it. As they came in sight Angelina grabbed a stone large enough to kill a man if it hit him on the head. I realized what she had in mind and wanted to join in but Angelina said, "Leave it to me!"

She threw the stone at the German who was walking alongside the prisoners, but deliberately aimed so as to miss him by a hair's breadth.

Her second stone hit. Massive confusion followed, which is what she had intended. One German was giving his attention to the wounded man; another tried to shoot but was disarmed in a matter of seconds. Eventually, under the impression that a large number of partisans were hiding up above, they simply ran away like hens before the fox.

That was when I first saw Angelina laugh. She leaned forward with her hands on her knees and was racked with quiet laughter that was more like sobbing.

By evening we were all reunited.

***

This was your Angelina, Sir, and ours. She was both courageous and clever.

⚜

At one time we were joined by an Englishman whom Antonio accepted. Angelina confided to me that she didn't like the man; he reminded her too much of a German in the SS.* I noticed that she kept a close eye on him, but without letting on that she suspected him. He spoke English fluently and without any accent.

One day Angelina put him to the test by suddenly speaking to him in German but it was quite obvious he didn't understand a word. I thought she was going to a lot of unnecessary trouble. After all, Antonio knew his people. But Angelina turned out to be right. One night she found him busy with a small wireless set — not one of ours. She woke Antonio, who had the man bound and tried to make him decode the secret news of the German High Command that he had been listening in to. When he refused, Antonio shot him before our very eyes! It was the first time Angelina saw that Antonio could kill.

---

*SS: the Schutzstaffel. The elite Nazi paramilitary force charged with protecting Hitler and eliminating threats to Nazi power. The SS was responsible for most of the atrocities committed by the Germans during World War II.

That night something happened between them that I guessed rather than saw, but it transpired that I had guessed right because Angelina afterwards told me about it. He tried to take her in his arms. He had never tried before and they had never spoken of love before; but it had come to that now and it was a dangerous hour. I now know that Angelina did love him, but she resisted him then and ever after.

(I should not have done so if I had been the one he wanted.)

From that night on Antonio avoided her and from that night on he seemed to lose his luck and his success.

※※◆◎◆○※※

At the beginning of November, Farinacci bombed the Vatican* and the next day we heard that the Germans were planning a huge attack on us. In my opinion Antonio ought to have laid low for a while, but he brushed aside the warning. The following night he dared to attack a troop train but was betrayed, pursued

---

*On November 5, 1943. Farinacci was an Italian who collaborated with the Nazis.

and driven into a mountain valley. There was a lot of shooting. We lost a third of our people that time. We had to abandon the wounded and each make our own way to safety.

I was very worried about Angelina. I couldn't find her anywhere and when all was quiet again and the Germans had withdrawn, I plucked up courage and went back to the valley with its dead and wounded.

One of the wounded men was dying and I couldn't help him. I dreaded finding Angelina dead or dying, but she was alive. I found her kneeling beside a man who had been shot in the gut and was constantly crying out for water. Although he was beyond hope, no one would have begrudged him a drink, only there was no water to be had anywhere near.

When Angelina realized it was me, she asked me a very odd question.

"Do you know how to pray?" she said.

Puzzled, I asked, "Why?"

"That man lying there," she whispered, "is Luigi, Tommaso's brother. I've had to promise that I will pray for him if he doesn't survive. But what can I pray? I don't know any prayers."

Naturally I could recall some prayers from

my childhood and I began to recite the *Pater Noster* and *Ave Maria*.* She remembered, and to make sure she wouldn't forget, she repeated these prayers from time to time. But Luigi looked like he would be a long time dying.

When he finally lost consciousness, Angelina tried to leave to get help, but when she wanted to take her hand out of Luigi's, he came to and wouldn't let her go. So she sent me off.

It was towards dawn. I thought I had heard a bell tolling and climbed upwards towards the sound. Each time I turned round and looked back into the valley, I saw Angelina still kneeling by Luigi. It started to rain and day dawned but there was no village to be seen. So I turned back.

In spite of the German presence, I wanted to risk going down into the plain, but Angelina wouldn't let me. She told me to wait until nightfall. So we stayed in that valley all day with our dead whom we couldn't bury, and the dying we couldn't help and who eventually died. Finally Luigi passed away, too. And, as she had promised, Angelina prayed the

---

*Pater Noster and *Ave Maria*: The Our Father and Hail Mary, prayed in Latin.

Pater Noster followed by the *Ave Maria*, and I whispered them with her.

It was dark when help came at last. Antonio came with the rest of them, and they started digging a grave for our dead.

Then something occurred that seemed like a dream although it was real; suddenly a priest stood there. No one knew who had fetched him. He blessed the grave with holy water and crucifix and incense, as he would have done in a graveyard. Antonio made the responses and the others prayed along. When the grave was covered over, the priest led us to the village and took us to his presbytery.

It was a very poor presbytery, the poorest I've ever seen. And when the priest brought us bread, apples and wine there was no doubt that he was sharing with us all he had.

We stayed with him overnight. Some of us slept in the kitchen and others in an empty sheep-pen, while a few kept watch outside the house. Antonio, Angelina and I stayed sitting with the priest.

He was still young, only a few years older than Antonio. He, too, was anti-Fascist and lived a life of poverty among the poor. We understood each other so well that Antonio felt able to ask if he would like to join us. The invitation was given in all seriousness and I noticed it was received in the same vein. He appeared to be genuinely pondering whether to come with us and in the end he said, "I will come with you, but only on one condition. You must stop killing."

Antonio asked if he believed Fascism could be destroyed without war, and war could be won without any killing. That was so true and so obvious that it was hard to see how it could be contradicted.

"War that is won by murder," said the priest, "will not bring you what you are hoping for."

It seemed Antonio was not to be beaten.

"Maybe not this war," he responded, "but we shall go on fighting and living in hope until justice and peace are established."

The priest said nothing and there was silence for a while until Antonio burst out: "It has got to happen in the end. It *will* come. It *must!*"

Silence returned but then he suddenly jumped up and, shaking the priest as if he were a tree, cried out, "Don't you believe it?"

The priest looked at him.

"My poor friend," he said quietly. "What you're fighting for will never come about."

Antonio let go of him so rapidly it looked as though he had pushed him against the wall.

"Never?" he repeated. "*Never*, you say? And how about that peace your God promised us, the people of good will? Can you deny that we're of good will? Aren't we the ones who are losing our lives to give life to those who come after us? Who could be more 'of good will' than we are?"

The priest gave him a look full of compassion and then said, "The peace you are talking about is not the same as the peace referred to there."

"A different kind, eh? A *different kind*!" cried Antonio. "I know all about that kind; your peace of soul, your spiritual satisfaction and your futile consolations."

The priest replied softly, "They are not futile."

But Antonio refused to hear him.

"And everything we're doing," he cried, "is supposed to be in vain? How *dare* you say that? How do you *know*?"

The priest didn't answer immediately. I could see by his expression he was struggling because he realized Antonio wouldn't be able to accept what he felt he must say. His face showed sadness and suffering, coupled with a humble conviction of being in the right.

What he said was, "The rule you want to help bring about cannot be established, because..."

"Cannot? Cannot?" Antonio broke in. "But it *must*! What are we supposed to do then? Put our hands in our laps and surrender our country to the Fascist dogs? Bequeath our children to exploiters? Wait until everything changes of its own accord? You fool! Can't you see earth's fate is in our hands? Can't you see we've been given a unique opportunity?"

When Antonio had stopped shouting, the priest, speaking so softly he could hardly be heard, said simply, "*My Kingdom is not of this world.*"

Antonio either *didn't* or *wouldn't* hear him.

"But you and your sort," he shouted, "are attacking us from the rear. You don't want progress because you're afraid of losing your power! Once the people no longer rely on your consolations and promises of life after death you'll be redundant and you know it. That's why you're against us."

The priest's smile was wise and compassionate and his voice gentle.

He addressed Antonio as if he were a naughty child.

"That's enough, Antonio. You're acting dumber than you really are. You know quite well that suffering can't be driven from the world by violence. Nor can it be wiped out by bread, work and welfare. You *do know* that, don't you? You yourself are full of tears that cannot be wiped away."

Antonio threw back his head.

"Don't bother," he said. "Keep it for your next sermon. It won't work on me."

The priest said nothing but looked very pale, and I shall never forget what happened next.

He held out his hand to Antonio and said, "I apologize. I wouldn't have dared to do what you've done. I've no right to judge. You're truly 'of good will' and I hope you find what you're looking for."

But Antonio ignored the hand held out to

him and looked away with an expression full of scorn. Then Angelina, who up to that point hadn't uttered a word, stood up and took the hand the priest was still offering.

"You're right," she said, "but he's also right. We have to act here and now. That is our truth. Right now we have no time to recognize any other."

I wanted her to have the last word. But the priest, who had seemed so mild, now spoke out, loudly and categorically, "There is no such thing as '*my* truth' or '*your* truth'," he said. "There is only *one* truth. You'll live to find that out."

There seemed nothing more to be said. His words sounded like a verdict.

Antonio laid a hand on Angelina's arm.

"Say nothing," he told her. "There's no point. He'll never understand us. He's not allowed to."

He turned to the priest.

"Listen," he said. "I was like you. I was studying theology. I used to talk and think the way you do, but I broke free. You should follow my example. You're fighting a losing battle. The future will sweep over you and your Church as if they didn't exist. Come with us! You'll find true life and a great task to live and die for. Forget your dream and open your eyes to reality."

The priest shook his head gently and was silent.

It was morning by then and time to set off. He stood on the threshold watching us go.

Suddenly Angelina burst out, "And we never even thanked him for the bread and wine and fruit, or for putting us up!"

She ran back, and I saw him smiling at her words (which we couldn't hear). Then, with his thumb, he made the sign of the cross on her forehead. I have no idea how she took it. I saw no reaction, and she said nothing about it later. Antonio said nothing either although he had seen what happened. Their day was full of tension and unease. I'm convinced they spent the whole of it carrying on a kind of wordless argument. And a shadow still hung over them in the days that followed.

Next we moved to somewhere near Manziana, where we had been before to bring the telephone wires down from the poles. They were down and lying on the ground as far as Bracciano. We heard that the Germans had asked the young people of Manziana to guard them, but none of them would because they had been told that if the line was in any way damaged, they would be shot.

So Antonio took five of his men and offered to stand guard. The Germans agreed and the people of Manziana were even more enthusiastic, because if anything occurred they could swear with a good conscience that it was nothing to do with them, and prove it.

Antonio mounted guard. I knew what was going to happen but I had no insight into what Angelina was planning, and I didn't hear about it until the day after, when we were already far away from Manziana, lying up in a safe hiding-place. I overheard it when Antonio was having a conversation with her, believing they were alone.

He was angry.

"You were not acting under my orders and I don't want you doing things off your own bat. And another thing...I don't want you doing anything that it's not your job to do. Either you stay and obey me, or you go."

Either Angelina gave him no answer, or else I didn't hear what she said.

"You don't have to prove to me that you're brave," he went on. "I take it for granted that everyone with me is that, do you understand?"

Again no reply.

His voice dropped.

"It would be much better if you went. This is no life for you. What will become of you?" And suddenly he was speaking loudly and harshly, "Go away *now*, *today*! Otherwise you'll be sorry you stayed."

At last she responded. I could hardly hear her and I realized just how agonizing all this was for her.

"Antonio," she said. "I don't know why you're treating me like this. I don't know what's really on your mind. And I've no idea where I'm supposed to go to. You're father, brother and friend to me! I want to stay with you."

After that there was a long silence.

Finally Antonio said, in a tone that was still harsh and must have hurt,

"Right then, stay. But never ever forget it was of your own free choice, and don't forget either that you're fighting for something which is not really you!"

"This *is* my cause," she replied, and there the conversation ended.

I think I now understand Antonio. He was in love with Angelina and his love gave him a sensitivity towards her that could detect her real self and true frame of mind. But she was so unreservedly loyal that she simply couldn't take in what he was trying to say.

Things started to get difficult after that, and it was especially hard for Angelina.

***

In the final week of that year, we were lying up between Alatri and Sora in an old but solidly constructed cowshed. We were having a quiet spell and doing our best to rest and recover our strength. But on New Year's Eve a heavy snowstorm blew up, so heavy that we were cut off from the rest of the world in minutes!

The storm blew the roof off and a falling tree knocked in the west wall. The cowshed was full of swirling snow and there was no shelter anywhere. We tried in vain to protect our transmitters, wireless sets and weapons with our bodies. It got colder and colder. The Italians were the first to start grumbling about the lot they had freely chosen. It was a dreadful night.

Towards morning, Antonio and another man went off to look for a better place to stay. They had tied planks to their feet and were able to 'ski' down into the valley.

Antonio had ordered us to stay there until he got back. Everyone set to repairing the shed and spent all day on it.

He didn't come back that day, nor in the night, nor the following day, and so a revolt started. Some said both of them must definitely have fallen into German hands, while others thought they must have frozen in the snow. A third opinion, not openly expressed, was that Antonio had grown tired of such a hopeless situation and had absconded. But everyone still went on sitting and waiting.

When a third day had gone by, however, and our food was running out, Pierino, one of the Italians, suddenly got to his feet. He said a decision had to be reached, and proceeded to tell us what it should be. The 'partisan war' he said, had become pointless, as the Allies would be landing any time now and our sacrifice would be wasted. Antonio had led us into paying a stupidly high price and what we had achieved was nothing when weighed in the balance of the war as a whole. He went on to say that Antonio must have realized this and abandoned us, so we ought to leave as well.

They all listened without a word but they were worn out, cold and hungry, and so one after the other they came to agree with Pierino. Some even started to move. And everyone was cursing Antonio.

What happened next was completely unexpected. Angelina stood blocking the doorway of the hut, carbine at the ready. She called out that they were all traitors and the first to go would be shot. I thought they would laugh and relieve her of the gun, which they could easily have done. But no one laughed and no one took her weapon. Silence fell.

Then Pierino yelled that he would shoot if she didn't move out of the doorway; and he raised his carbine, too.

I still can't believe he would have shot her. He just wanted to scare her. But the minute he raised his weapon there was a shot from behind and Pierino was hit. I didn't know who had fired the shot and afterwards it was never mentioned. I do know now, of course.

Pierino's body was carried away and tossed into the ravine, after which they all went back into the hut and waited on in silence.

***

Antonio arrived in the evening with provisions and news. He asked after Pierino but no one said anything. Later on one of them took him aside and told him what had happened.

I was with Angelina the whole time and know that Antonio never discussed the event with her. I had the impression he was proud of her and yet furious with her, and I couldn't understand his attitude because, if it hadn't been for her, the group would have been dissolved that day. I have come to believe that he couldn't approve of her action without making her feel responsible for a man's death. He and all the rest were allowed to kill, but Angelina wasn't.

The next day we climbed down lower and were able to make it to the valley unhindered. Snow had smothered the war. The Germans' cars were buried in it, looking like small snow-covered hills. Electricity lines were not working, torn off their masts and hanging or lying everywhere. We saw no Germans. Instead we soon met plenty of refugees coming towards us down the narrow roads between high walls of snow.

Then, on January 7th, we had a bomb attack and that night the moon shone down on the dead by the side of the road.

***

The following weeks were bad. We suffered repeated attacks from bombers and 'hedge-hoppers'. We helped in the villages, hiding the dead and wounded and chasing away grief.

On January 22nd we heard that the Allies had landed in Anzio, and consequently refugees arrived in far greater numbers than we could ever have anticipated. They wanted to go to Rome, only to Rome, as Rome had been declared a free city. We, on the other hand, moved off southwards against the flow of refugees and by the 26th we were nearer to the front line than ever before.

***

And now, Sir, I've reached the part of my story I should like to have spared you, because it will upset you. But how would it help you not to have the full and true story of what happened? So for Angelina's sake, and for the sake of the truth that is greater than ourselves and our desires, please follow me in the strength of whatever love for her you can find in your heart.

***

January 26th 1944 was the day that changed Angelina's life with one stroke. That was the day we were parted, but I was with her up to the very moment when it happened.

The snow had melted, the weather was dull, and under cover of dusk we were slowly working our way up a narrow cleft to a point halfway up a mountain. If it hadn't been so dark and we hadn't been so exhausted, we should have recognized this mountain.

The German Command had taken up its quarters in a large farmhouse just halfway up.

Some days before, we had met up with another group of partisans who had hand grenades. The Germans believed they were secure and were therefore unprepared. They were asleep.

The guards were quickly dealt with and our party threw the grenades. But our information was lacking. It turned out there was someone hidden below the house and we were answered with machine-gun fire. We had to run away, and were forced uphill until we eventually found cover in a ruin on the other side of the mountain. And we began shooting from there.

I say 'we', Sir, but that does not include me. The rest *were* shooting, however, and for the first time Angelina was as well. She was standing on a wall shooting. I have no idea whether she actually shot anyone, but she later claimed she *had* and that the pain of knowing she had killed someone would never go away.

I lost sight of her just then. She vanished and, as we had to flee, I thought she must have run ahead. But when we all met up again some hours after, Angelina was not there. She was the only one missing from Antonio's group.

Antonio was beside himself, and although the mountain was occupied by the Germans he set off in broad daylight to look for her. He came back during the night without having found her.

After that he tried several times to go back to the mountain but eventually gave up hope. From then on, he hardly spoke a word and we began to be afraid of him.

***

In April we all separated. Tommaso and I stayed, with another man from our group, at his parents' home near Velletri. Then one day I heard Antonio was badly wounded somewhere near Frosinone, no one knew quite where. But the news was enough to startle me into setting out to look for him. It was absolute madness running off straight into the war like that, but I did and nothing would stop me.

In the end I never found Antonio at all. Instead, by some strange means, I found Angelina!

Afterwards I wondered why I hadn't realized from the start where she might — indeed *must* — be. Maybe it would have dawned on me at once if I hadn't been misled. You see, when I asked the name of the place where we had last seen Angelina, I was given several different answers, and even hearing its proper name failed to jog my memory. This is understandable when you think what disturbing times we were living in. But what I *needed* to find I *found*!

On the way to Frosinone I saw a mountain rising straight from the plain as many do round there. But there was no town on the top as there were on all the rest, only a heap of ruins.

All at once I remembered — not the night when we had entrenched ourselves up there and lost Angelina. No, what came back to me was the time when the two of us had stood down where I was now, with Angelina trembling while we watched this town being bombarded.

I'm sure it was not my reason that impelled me to climb up to that ruined place. After all what could I expect to find there except ruins?

The little town was quite dead, and deserted by all its inhabitants.

I clambered around among the ruins and found no sign of any person living there. The first sound I heard was the cackling of hens behind a wall.

I climbed up on the wall and saw a garden that had clearly been destroyed, but showed signs of someone's having recently made efforts to restore it. And I saw someone working there, a nun in a black habit, with a white scarf tied around her head like a peasant woman. She was quite alone.

Some loose stones rolled down and gave me away, making her look up. At first she didn't seem surprised to see someone and even smiled, but as soon as she saw it was me she was startled and then it was my turn to be struck dumb — it was Angelina! The meeting was so unexpected we must both have thought we were seeing things.

Angelina was the first to recover, which is not hard to understand because she was seeing me as she was used to seeing me. But how was *I* supposed to recognize *her* in the habit of a nun? When she called out my name I felt quite shy about approaching her, but she helped put me at my ease.

As you will have guessed, this was Santa Maria del Monte and the garden belonged to the convent, a Benedictine abbey, which like the rest of the place had been destroyed and abandoned. Only the chapel was left standing, with little damage; and the choir, and half the refectory.

She showed it all to me, referring to '*my* convent', '*my* chapel', '*my* garden', '*my* hens'. She was all alone there and had been in that place for three months; alone in the deserted town, alone in the abandoned convent. I could hardly take it in.

***

But then she told me the whole story right from the beginning and this is what I'm passing on to you, Sir, quite simply, just as I first heard it.

I wish you could have heard it as I did then in Angelina's quiet, frail voice, the voice of someone who was not trying to hide anything but had almost forgotten how to share.

⁂

We sat in the convent garden where hens were scratching around in freshly-dug beds. Aircraft flew low over us, and down in the valley the trucks rolled and the refugees streamed. We were right in the middle of the war and yet far removed from it. And we were still sitting there when darkness fell.

The day we thought we had lost Angelina she had tumbled backwards off a crumbling wall, just after firing a shot. She had fallen quite a long way down and been covered with rubble. She lay down there in some vaulted cellars for goodness knows how long until she regained consciousness.

By the time she came to, the blood from her many wounds had already clotted. They were not bad wounds but both her feet were sprained and she had torn tendons in both legs. She couldn't walk, only crawl.

She crawled her way out of the rubble and through the cellars until she found a cistern of clean water and some food — a little wine and oil, maize and some onions. She ate and drank, and then went to sleep.

When she woke up she crawled farther and came into the garden where she found spinach and a kind of turnip. She heard a rooster crowing in the distance, thought there were people in the place and expected to come across them before long. She was quite confident, just tired. She guessed she had had a concussion and so kept very quiet and slept in her cellar as much as she could.

When her head finally cleared she saw it was spring. It must have been February. The sky was blue, and a light breeze wafted the scent of herbs.

Her legs were starting to obey her again, and now she began to explore the rest of the house attached to the cellar where she had found shelter. She discovered a kitchen with a stone hearth and pans, and found a stair leading up to a long corridor with lots of doors on one side. On the other side were empty holes for windows, through which you could see the valley far down below.

The passage had lost its roof and the doors were stuck because they were blocked from behind with rubble. The only door that would open was right at the end and led into a room separated from a larger room by metal bars. These were the choir and the chapel and both still had a roof. The roofs had been held up and kept intact by thick, four-sided pillars bowed with age but still strong enough to support them.

This part of the house and the tiny sacristy were the only habitable space and Angelina lived there. The sacristy was her bedroom. In a cupboard there she had found some old carpets and a cloth she didn't know the purpose of. She had used these for bedding.

There was also a thick wax candle only half burned down — the Paschal candle. By its light she had spent night after night reading the only book she had been able to find: a Benedictine breviary.

"A beautiful and uplifting book..." (I remember her exact words.) "You ought to read it, too," she told me, as if this was quite a natural thing to say. She had no idea how hard it was to take in finding her here, surrounded by all this.

I realize now that she did the right thing, simply drawing me into her world rather than offering explanations. One should never attempt to explain the truth or one's powerful experiences. These are to be lived so that others will one day understand.

⚜

So I'm asking you, too, Sir, to understand without any explanation from me. How could I ever explain, for instance, what Angelina must have gone through the day she found a small box of Hosts in the sacristy and, without knowing whether or not they were consecrated, experienced joy, and another strange, new feeling that made her place the vessel on the altar and leave it there?

It is time to return to my story, or rather your daughter's.

⚜

The concussion caused by her fall continued

to affect her for some time and she lived a dreamlike existence. Being very close to the front, she couldn't help hearing the thunder of artillery and the rattle of machine-guns, but she lived as though the war no longer concerned her. In the daytime, when she sat in the garden, aircraft swooped so low over her that the pilots could easily have seen Angelina and maybe did, but neither they nor the advancing army below gave any thought to the ruined town.

There came a day when Angelina's senses were quite restored and it was a difficult awakening. She found a carbine in the cellar and recognized it as hers. She suddenly remembered that she had fired a shot and had very likely hit someone. This had slipped her mind, but now the memory came back and she started searching for the dead man. She knew in what direction she had aimed and that her victim, if there was one, must either be lying below the outer wall of the convent or have rolled down the almost vertical mountainside and landed in a cleft. There seemed little chance of finding him, but she went on and on searching, and in the end she found him; at least she found *a* dead German already in a state of decay.

Angelina's bullet might or might not have hit this man and her reason told her that he couldn't really be *her* victim because he must have been lying there for more than just a few weeks. But she felt what she realized was a disproportionate sense of responsibility.

After she had covered the dead man with fresh olive branches and stones, she sat down by the little mound and tried to shake off her low spirits. She told herself everything that someone else would probably have said to reason her into a happier frame of mind, especially that she couldn't be sure she had shot *this* man or indeed *anyone*, and that in any case she had only done her duty in an emergency as was proper in wartime. She used other such arguments and told herself she had killed in support of a great ideal. But her own words didn't convince her. For someone as alone as Angelina was, there were no excuses. There lay a dead man and even if he was not *her* dead man she had been *prepared* to kill this man (or another). Whether her shot had gone home or not made no difference. The commandment "Thou shalt not kill" had no limits and applied in all circumstances.

Angelina was trembling as she said this. I felt for her with all my heart.

"A person can't be held guilty if they don't know a thing is forbidden," I said, trying to calm her.

But she cried out, "That is *untrue*! It is absolutely and totally untrue. If you're ignorant of something then the guilt lies precisely in your ignorance. It is there to be known, anyone can know, only they act as if they were blind and deaf."

To take her mind off this confession which had so upset her I asked, "So what did you do *then*?" I was hoping she would go on to tell me how she had set about getting the garden in order again but her mind was still on the same subject.

"Then?" she answered. "Then I swore an oath: I swore from that day on to love all and to make retribution for everything I had done. And with that in mind I decided to leave and look for some useful work to do. I was planning to become a nurse and afterwards, in peacetime, do more study to become a doctor and work among the poor."

"Then why," I asked, "did you not leave?"

"I was not allowed to."

"You were not allowed to? But there was no one to stop you!"

She didn't answer. Instead, she unhesitatingly turned to look and point straight at a nearby gateway. What I saw was an arch with some ancient writing engraved on it. It said: *Egredere si potes*. 'Leave, if you can.'

I didn't understand. How could I?

"And that was what kept you here?" I asked stupidly.

Angelina gave a little smile.

"The full version goes: '*egredere modo, frater, egredere si potes*'* and it was spoken by a sister to her brother after she had begged him to stay all night and pray with her because she knew she was about to die. But the brother told her he must go home to his monastery, whereupon the sister began to beseech God to send a heavy rainstorm, heavy enough to make her brother

---

*"Just leave, brother, leave if you can."

stay. God sent the rain out of love for her and that is when she said: 'Now, leave if you can!'"

I laughed because I thought it a pretty story about a clever woman whose cunning not even God could resist.

But Angelina responded: "That was no cunning; that was *trust*. They were the holy sister and brother, Saint Scholastica and Saint Benedict."

I still couldn't understand how the ancient inscription had had the power to keep Angelina there.

***

And now, Sir, I'm going to have to tell you something you will not be happy about, something you will put down to pure chance.

***

After your daughter had made up her mind to leave, and was already on the threshold (or rather the place under the rubble where the threshold must have been), she suddenly remembered the vessel containing the Hosts and didn't want to leave it there unprotected. So she turned and went back into the chapel intending to put it in a niche in the wall.

Now she was ready to go, but when she stood on the threshold for the second time she slipped and sprained a foot, the one that was not quite healed — and so couldn't walk.

This was the day, she told me, when she started to talk with God as a presence beside her.

She spoke to Him angrily and said, "It was for Your sake I turned back, to save the Bread You say is your Flesh. And You thank me by letting me fall over and sprain my foot!"

She also told Him He would be fooling Himself if He thought He could keep her here by force. And she let Him know that she didn't believe in Him, but then began to be afraid she was going crazy, because it seemed crazy to talk to a being that didn't exist.

That night, the night after she had found the dead man, must have been terrible for her. She couldn't sleep for the pain, and to shorten the long night, she lit the Easter candle and began to flick through the pages of the only book she could find. It was the breviary in

Latin and she tried to translate it.

The first sentence that caught her eye was, 'The snare is broken and I am free.' This sentence pierced her like an arrow, and was followed immediately by another. Inscribed in the front of the book was the name of the person to whom the book belonged:

Maria Angela — for her Profession
6 May 1823

Angelina had been given the names 'Maria Angela' when she was baptized, and although you could call it a genuine coincidence, Angelina didn't find it so that night, and is now even less inclined to think of it as such.

Written below the original date there is now another: 24 July 1947. The name is the same because Angelina was allowed to keep that name, and the breviary as well.

That first Maria Angela had become the Abbess of Maria del Monte and was renowned for her saintly life. In the bottom right-hand corner of the title page, she had written, in tiny letters, the following words:

'*Inveni, quem diligit anima mea.*'

'I have found Him Whom my soul loveth.'

The fine pencil line under these words was put there by Angelina, but only long after.

That night she had no thought of underlining anything in the breviary. She simply intended to pass the time with it and practice her Latin.

But she soon found the book had started something there was no stopping. It became a source of deep confusion, confronting her like a well-armed opponent and a secret judge. The book dared to say:

The bow of the mighty shall be broken and the weak shall be girded with strength. Those who once ate in plenty will go short of bread: the hungry shall be fed. The Lord deals out poverty and riches. The Lord is judge to the ends of the earth.

Angelina showed me the place and asked me if I knew what it meant. I thought it was easy to understand. The God referred to is on the side of the poor and the oppressed. He puts down the rich and helps the poor to get their rights.

"Yes," she said. "That is what I thought too,

at the time. I also thought that, if this was so, we must be fighting on God's side, but then I thought that what was being said about this God couldn't be right because where was He in our battle? If He were really on our side He should have given us the victory *long* ago. And I thought the world had been in existence long enough to give God time to bring everything into good order. It seemed clear to me that God had failed. But why? Either He was not just and not almighty, or else He didn't want to meddle with our freedom, in which case the verse of the psalm had got it wrong. Or alternatively, He didn't want to side with us because our sort of thing was not His and might be bad."

It occurred to me that Angelina had missed another possibility and I said: "Didn't you think that this God might not even exist?"

"No," she said. "I couldn't think that. He had become real to me, so real that I talked to Him as if he was with me, and He *was*, too! The way I talked to Him was pure blasphemy. I was furious with Him and embittered. I told Him he was an unjust and cruel God and ought not to be surprised if we who were created in His image were unjust and cruel. I said more than that, things I can't repeat. At that time, I not only said all that but I shouted it aloud until it echoed round the chapel — until I was afraid of myself and of God whom I had challenged in this way. But you know, Giulia, I'm sure He understood me. He didn't mind me quarrelling with Him like that. It was my first real prayer. It was the first time I experienced His existence. He was my only partner then and has been ever since." Her final words were spoken quickly and quietly, and then she held her breath, upset at having divulged her secret.

She jumped up at once and muttered something about having to shut up the hens. She rounded them all up, the six or seven hens and the rooster, as expertly as a farmer's wife and shooed them into a wooden coop she had made herself.

When she came back she told me the hens didn't belong to her, but whoever really owned them, she had found them wandering around the place on their own and had caught them; and they were laying a lot of eggs.

But all the time she was chattering on, her mind must still have been on the piece from the psalm and in the end she asked me straight out:

"Don't you think that what is being said in the psalm is meant to be taken differently?"

"How, then?" I asked. Instead of answering she read me the passage again. "Now," she said. "Did you hear?"

I was not used to such thoughts and it went against the grain that Angelina should be stubbornly trying to make clear to me something that didn't concern me. So I told her with some impatience that I hadn't a clue what to make of it.

Emphatically, yet with forbearance, she answered, "It says here that it is the Lord who establishes justice. It is *the Lord* who brings down the rich and helps the poor. Yet we presume to do what *He alone* can do! What is being said is so clear, that one wonders how it could ever be misunderstood!"

This was too much for me. I replied that in that case we should have to leave it entirely to Him to put the world straight, while we sat with our hands in our laps, but that is not how it works at all. If we *must* talk about God all the time then all we could say is that in every case it is our strength He uses to bring about order.

"Order? Order?" cried Angelina in a voice that was unusually severe. "What we think of as 'order' might possibly be *dis*order! But," she went on, with a sudden return to gentleness, "I was merely trying to tell you what a tussle I had with that book, which was the only one in this house, the only one in the whole place, and had so many upsetting things of that sort to say. Yet there are others: consoling, beautiful and full of sweetness."

I didn't want to hear any more of all that, and to turn her attention to something else I dared to step in where she might still feel vulnerable.

"I came into this region," I said, "because someone told me Antonio might be lying here somewhere. I came to look for him." I saw Angelina go pale and I was sorry to have given her such a shock.

"He's not dead," I told her. "He's wounded and is supposed to be in hospital somewhere round here. But I've not so far managed to find him." She didn't say a word.

"Do you want to come with me and help look for him?" I asked.

Still no response apart from a scarcely visible shake of her head. Then she looked at me earnestly with her clear eyes, trying to make me realize how stupid I had been to ask this question.

But I only got some of the message, not enough to stop me asking, "So does that mean you've deserted him completely?"

She turned away from me and stared straight ahead, though not at anything in particular. But I took in her stony expression and the way she pressed her hands together, and saw that she had gone white and rigid.

I didn't dare say any more. The muffled sound of the war coming up to us from the valley seemed suddenly louder. The peace of the convent garden was broken. The wind rose, driving away the bees with their soft familiar droning, and it felt chilly.

Yet Angelina quickly pulled herself together. That was what I had always admired about her — her way of becoming what you might call 'detached from her own self'. Although she was still looking pale she said, "Is it too cold for you? Shall we go in?" I was frozen, but not in a way that could easily be dealt with. I was frozen on account of her decision.

"Let's stay here," I said.

Angelina took off a piece of black cloth that she had wrapped twice round her shoulders and tied in a knot beneath her chest. It was the scapular that she had used in this way, not knowing what it was for. I didn't know either when Angelina put it round my shoulders to keep me a bit warmer. I wanted to ask why she was wearing the habit and whether it meant anything, but I didn't have the courage to ask any more questions.

Then she volunteered an answer. "This is all I have to wear," she said. "What I was wearing was torn to shreds. I found these clothes when I started to tidy up in the cells. You see, I'm trying to make it possible to live in a cell that still has half its roof, and while I was clearing away the rubble I came across a smashed-in cupboard with this in it and some underclothes and various other items a nun is allowed to have. I'm expecting to find more as time goes on. I think the nuns must have fled in a fearful hurry and taken only what was absolutely necessary. If you could help me dig here…" She interrupted herself. "What a ridiculous thing to say! Of course you won't want to stay here in this nest amongst the rubble."

I didn't actually, and I thought Angelina wouldn't want to either, but all I said was, "I'll stay a few days if you'll have me."

I was not so sure Angelina would want to keep me with her. I felt like an intruder. I was disturbing her beautiful, harsh solitude. She did later confide that she had hoped I would go away again soon, as I was preventing her from carrying on her intimate converse with the One she called her 'only true partner'.

***

Angelina started her real convent life then. The fact is, convent life does not allow for much solitude or freedom and that is hard, hardest of all for such a solitary being as she was. I'm the only one who knows how much she has suffered, and still does, from having to live in community. The more she suffers, the kinder she gets, and the kinder she gets, the more people make claims on her. And the greater her love, the more she is tormented.

It was just like that then, when I was disturbing her and yet stayed because she was so good to me. I was her first novice, but she didn't know it and neither did I. And if you, Sir, find it impossible to understand how Angelina can suffer and at the same time not want to leave, all I can say is this: she stays of her own free will, and no one ought to try and touch upon her secret. Despite it all, she's happy.

<hr />

Just as we reached this stage in our conversation that first evening, a small figure suddenly appeared on top of the wall at the spot where I had climbed in several hours before. It was a young boy about eleven years old. Angelina smiled across at him the way she had done at me.

"Come on then," she called and he jumped down like a cat without losing anything out of the basket he was carrying.

"Who is that, Sister?" he asked, full of

mistrust at the sight of me.

"She's one of us," Angelina said, throwing me into confusion. She noticed and said, "Don't worry. This is Francesco. He calls me 'Sister' because I'm wearing this habit but he knows who I really am. Francesco is the youngest brother of Alfonso, if you remember him. He was the one who shot Pierino." This information was given without hesitation as if we were still together in the group and were speaking about a burning issue of general concern. I began to hope that she might still find her way back to us, and my hope grew as she listened to Francesco telling her the latest news of the war and seemed bitterly disappointed that there had been no marked progress.

It was the end of April. The Germans were holding the front in the south-west and it looked as though they would hang on to it for goodness knows how long.

For many weeks Francesco had been the only human being Angelina saw. The youngster lived in the valley. Since he had made friends with her, having met her when his goats had strayed on the mountain, he had been coming two or three times a week to bring bread and cheese and news, in exchange for the eggs laid by Angelina's hens.

Long afterwards she admitted to me that it was through him she first heard Antonio had been wounded. What a severe temptation I must have put her through when I tried to persuade her to look for Antonio, after she had held out for so long! (But this was not the last test, nor the hardest.)

When Francesco had gone I asked her to carry on with her story. She had decided by then not to reveal any more of her secret. Instead she described how she had made the place comfortable to live in.

One day, in the rubble that was all that remained of a nearby building, she had discovered some garden tools and a small box of seeds. She began digging and sowing. The seeds were in tiny cloth bags with no writing on them, so when she put them in the ground she hadn't a clue what they would grow into.

She pointed out the beds that were now showing green and revealing what was growing from those seeds. "We should both have enough to eat if you wanted to stay," she said. When I didn't answer, however, she straightway switched to talking about something else that seemed harmless enough. Yet it was clear every thought, of any kind whatsoever, brought her back in some strange way to her one great theme. This led her into relating what she had been doing in the evenings.

The days were longer and the evenings warmer. She found less need for sleep. She had recovered. Once she had finished her daytime work in the garden and had prepared her one hot meal, she would sit by one of the empty windows in the convent corridor and read. She read her one and only book and perused psalm after psalm.

I imagine not one of Saint Benedict's children has ever been engaged in such a hard struggle as she was, reading the breviary and allowing it to lead her through a kind of martyrdom because she wouldn't admit to herself how excited she was by this strange, great world she had entered.

And that brought us back again to what was really preoccupying her.

"Then," she said, "I discovered the cursing

psalms. They're dreadful. One of them starts with these truly beautiful and extremely sad words, *'By the waters of Babylon we sat down and wept'* and ends with a curse on the Edomites, *'Blessed be the one who takes your children and dashes them on the rocks.'* Not even when the Fascists took my father, have I ever wished anything so frightful! Perhaps the interpretation should be different. I hardly understand any of it yet."

I dared to voice an objection.

"Ah, but you see that is from the Old Testament where revenge was seen as justice and was good and permitted."

"Yes," she said, "but the Benedictines, and maybe Catholic priests as well, read this now, *now* in *our* day when what matters is the commandment to love."

"Ah," I said, feeling this was all grist to the mill. "We have to realize that this commandment no longer counts for much in today's Church. Since the Church got mixed up in politics it has learned to hate, curse its enemies, and bless the weapons that will kill the fathers of the children in the enemy camp."

Angelina said nothing but her face wore a pained expression as if I had hurt her deeply.

Ignoring this I said, "Well, isn't it true? My father always used to say he would become a Christian without delay if only the Church was the way Christ intended it to be."

Angelina was compelled to answer this challenge.

She said softly, "It looks as if you could be right."

I was more upset by her *"it looks as if"* than I would have been had she contradicted me. I was beginning to realize that Angelina had already started to feel at home in a world I no longer approved of. She was suffering because this 'world' was not as it should be. She suffered out of love; yet couldn't bear anyone to point out the weaknesses in what was now dear to her.

Later, when I too had found this love, though maybe not as ardent a love as hers, we often discussed this difficult question, and Angelina made me realize that the Church's weakness is the test of how strong our faith and loyalty is. This weakness is imposed so that, time and again, the Church's existence over two thousand years can be proved to be the result not of *its merit* but of *grace*. The plan of salvation was designed this way from the beginning.

That evening we knew nothing of all that, yet I believe Angelina anticipated it when she said, "Christ was crucified, and at the time he died had achieved nothing in this world."

I was not familiar with all this, and this sort of talk made me uncomfortable.

I was embarrassed by her preoccupation with these questions — questions that seemed to me divorced from reality. It even crossed my mind she might have incurred some brain damage when she fell into the cellar.

My suspicion increased when she told me that one day she had started praying and singing aloud the Hours.* She had found an introduction to the singing of the psalms when she was clearing away the rubble. There was music with it and she had spent ages learning it. It was plainsong, though, and very hard to learn unless you were trained in it. We found that out a few months later when we heard it

---

Hours: The Monastic Office — services prayed in the community at set hours of the day and night.

sung properly. Angelina had to work hard on 'unlearning' the mistakes she had taken such trouble to memorize.

That first evening she told me she had found another little book one day, tattered, mildewed and incomplete. She was carrying it in her pocket and showed it me: 'The Rule of St. Benedict'. I leafed through it and read a bit of it. I found it dry, boring and meaningless, and I handed it back to her. She looked at me expectantly, but what could I say? I didn't understand a word of it.

She gave a little smile and tucked the book carefully and tenderly away as if it were something precious.

"It makes such wonderful sense," she said.

I couldn't see that at all, and I was glad when the noise of the aeroplanes overhead got so loud that for a while we couldn't hear ourselves think.

When it was quiet again, and I was hoping the planes had taken Angelina's mind off the subject, she said, "Do you remember how once when we were children my *nonna* and your mother took us to Assisi? There was a tiny convent there, a very poor one on the edge of the town. And there were nuns. We heard them singing or praying, I can't remember which. You and I were in the courtyard of the convent, sitting on the stones. There were white doves and trees with huge leaves that rustled in the wind; and we heard the Sisters singing. Do you remember?"

I did remember. The convent was San Damiano. I also remembered how Angelina sat there stock still with her hands folded, and how, when her grandmother called her she didn't want to come, and how she cried when they forced her to come away. I knew, but I didn't admit it to Angelina. I said there was more than one convent around Perugia we had been to — but she was not really listening.

"I remember asking Nonna," she said, "whether nuns prayed all day, and her telling me they had fixed times for prayer. In this little book it says they pray seven times a day, once at night, but I don't know exactly when."

"What do you need to know for?" I asked. "You're not a nun, even if those clothes do make you look like one."

"No," she agreed. "I'm not a sister. But when I divide the day by the Hours it gives it a certain order."

To my mind, order came through more natural means; why else wear watches? Or, as Angelina no longer had one, how about the course of the sun?

"That's a different kind of order," she said, smiling. She wanted to leave it there but I persisted, even though I didn't really care either way.

"Tell me," I asked. "How did you come to start praying these Hours?"

"I just started," she replied. "It was like a game, a serious game with strict rules. I've always liked living within an ordered framework but I've always had to create one for myself."

"A game!" I said. "A game and an adventure. And when you've finished playing and the adventure no longer appeals?"

She gave me a pitying look and made no reply.

The game had long ceased to be a game and it dawned on me that the whole thing was much deeper and more important to her than Angelina had let me see.

"You really *are* living like a nun? *You,*

Angelina! Whatever has come over you? This place has bewitched you. There's something here that has you caught in a web. You're under a spell and no longer yourself. You have to get away from here quickly, as quickly as you can."

I had jumped up, frightened and agitated, but Angelina pulled me gently back down on to the stone we were using as a seat.

"You're right," she said. "I'm not the person I was. But don't you think that up to now I was not myself, and that now for the first time I'm myself and clear-sighted and sensible?"

"Sensible?" I cried. "Do you call it sensible to be sitting all alone in a ruined convent, singing Latin prayers in plainsong, weeding the garden and carrying on crazy conversations with a non-existent being? Sensible! If you were sensible you would come with me and do some really sensible work, work that would benefit others. There is a lot to do down there in the valley."

I saw that I had touched a spot but she answered me quietly. "That is what I tell myself every day, but..." And she pointed again to the inscription over the gateway.

I gave up arguing with her. "All right, then," I said. "You've restored the garden and begun to shift the rubble out of one of the cells. What else are you planning to do?"

"Oh," she said. "That will be made clear. Antonio taught me how to be obedient."

"But there is nobody here to tell you what to do!" I cried, suddenly feeling that Angelina must surely have lost her reason.

Her answer was quite clear. "Under whose obedience did you pick out this mountain from among many others and climb it? And whom did we obey when we set out that time and simply kept on going until we ended up in Rome?"

I acknowledged myself beaten, but actually only to get away from these discussions. This time it worked, and the rest of the evening passed very peacefully. We ate the bread and cheese Francesco had brought, and Angelina still had a little wine as well — rather sour but it was a treat to have wine at all.

We sat outside until late at night. Then Angelina led me into the sacristy, which was her bedroom. It was stuffy in there and smelled of old masonry and mice but she was used to it. She was expecting me to have her bed.

But these were all the blankets there were. There was nothing else to lie on. "And how about you?" I queried. "Where are *you* going to sleep?"

There was a thick carpet in front of the altar in the chapel. "Why don't we take that?" I suggested.

"That?" Angelina sounded upset. "But we can't take anything from the altar!"

"Well why not, when we're so cold? And anyway it's no longer an altar." I went up the steps. Naturally the consecration stone* had gone. "You see," I said. "Your nuns took the stone with them. Without it the altar is no longer an altar. I remember enough to be sure about that anyway."

I was really sorry I'd said that when I saw how upset and disappointed Angelina was, but I couldn't take it back and I had told her the honest truth.

"Right, then," she whispered. "That means we can take the carpet." While she was rolling it up she said something I didn't understand.

Consecration stone: a slab of natural stone set into an altar upon which the Eucharistic sacrifice is offered during Mass.

"What's that you're saying?" I asked.

"Oh, nothing in particular," she answered in embarrassment. Then with some effort she added, "I was praying for forgiveness."

"Whose forgiveness?" I asked, astonished. But then I realized. I was highly uncomfortable about such dealings with someone I certainly believed in but was not in the habit of speaking to.

In the end we both had something to lie down on and I was asleep in next to no time.

***

Some time later Angelina woke me. There was a noise going on that sounded like shells landing on rock. There were sharp crashes that no one who has heard them can ever forget. We stood up and saw the area to the south-east of Maria del Monte lit up with what looked like prolonged flashes of lightning. It was a huge number of flares and we could see they were focussed on a steep, high mountain separated by a considerable gap from the main range and standing as if it had been pushed out into the valley.

"That must be Monte Cassino!" Angelina said, sounding absolutely horrified.

I had only seen Monte Cassino in pictures. I knew that the huge, ancient edifice was built on a high, steep mountain that, if properly defended, had to be unassailable. But now, under such fierce attack from the air, it was exposed and practically defenceless.

Why was the monastery being attacked anyway, and who were its attackers? Judging by the sound of the engines, and the stage the war had reached, it could only be the Allies. There was just one explanation. The German military must have taken it over.

Angelina didn't agree. She thought an Italian monastery could never have been occupied by German forces. But what if the abbot had no choice? What if the monks had already paid for their resistance with their lives?

Who could have known how near the mark Angelina was when she said that this attack must either be a mistake or the result of treason? "Any Germans in the monastery," she said, "would have returned fire, and we should have been able to see signs of it and hear the shooting."

In fact we sat there hearing no response. Monte Cassino lay silent and let itself be destroyed. Witnessing this event was unbearable.

Angelina saw it was making me ill. "Go and sleep," she said, sympathetically.

"And how about you?" I asked.

"Go on," she said. "I'll come in a while."

I lay awake a long time and she didn't come. At dawn, when I eventually got up to look for her I found her on her knees in the convent corridor, her eyes fixed on the holy mountain. She didn't hear me.

If she was storming heaven that time, asking for Monte Cassino to be saved, her prayer was certainly not heard.

From that night on the noise of the war was incessant. Monte Cassino had become the focus of the front. If the monastery had in reality been empty of Germans when it was attacked, the mountain and the whole surrounding area were soon full of them and they were engaged in a bitter struggle. It was clear to us that the Allies had used their beachhead to cordon off the whole of the south and that Cassino was the last barrier preventing them from pushing rapidly ahead towards Rome. The capture of Cassino was going to be the turning-point of the war. But Cassino didn't fall. We waited day after day and night after night.

Angelina had stopped working in the garden. She could hardly be made to eat. We took it in turns to keep watch at night as if we were attending a sickbed — of someone whose death we dreaded enormously, yet longed for as a merciful release.

We had to wish final victory on the Allies, including victory over Monte Cassino. But how could we wish the monastery destroyed? Angelina already looked on it as St. Benedict's monastery, 'home patch', holy ground. And for me — as for all Italians, whether devout or not — it was a place with a tradition, a place to be proud of. Once, Angelina asked me if I still wanted to be fighting on the side of the Allies.

May was hot. The charred and damaged acacias had put out new shoots, and in war as in peace, bloomed as they had always done with a sweet scent that was overpowering. For no reason that I could put my finger on I grew sadder by the day.

Angelina noticed it and in the end she said,

"You go! You can't stand much more of this life."

"You come, too," I said.

She shook her head, gentle but determined.

Her quiet obstinacy maddened me. "What do you want to do here?" I asked. "After all, you can't stay here forever."

"Why not?" she said in all seriousness.

"Why *not*?" I cried, and prepared to play my highest card. "Have you forgotten what you told the nuns in that convent near Rieti? Have you forgotten you said they were cowards and deserters, leading useless lives?"

"No," she said. "I have not forgotten."

"Well?" I retorted angrily.

"I didn't know then what I know now," she said.

"And what *is* it you're claiming to have found out?"

"Oh, nothing very much," she answered with a little smile that made me feel embarrassed. "It's simply that..." and she broke off unable to put into words what filled her heart to overflowing. Then she said quickly, as if she had moved on to something else and was now having a bit of a joke, "It's just the old story of the magnetic mountain."

"What magnetic mountain?"

"The one in *The Thousand and One Nights*. You know, a mountain that turns out to be a magnet and attracts everything made of iron. Every ship that comes near is lost."

I remembered then. "Yes," I said. "And you *really are* lost! In fact you've been *shattered* on that mountain."

"Yes," was all she said.

Every conversation now ended in the same way. I felt that I had all the sensible arguments on my side. And yet Angelina was right, against all the odds and despite not caring about winning. She just conceded, simply and gently. And as I was not really argumentative by nature and no good at discussions, nearly all our conversations were inconclusive, light as spiders' threads left hanging in mid-air.

<hr/>

But I'm forgetting, Sir, that I'm writing for you, not myself. I've been lost in my memories.

We were forced to look on at the death struggle of Monte Cassino for three whole weeks. But on the 21st of May the holy mountain fell quiet and on the 22nd our trustworthy young reporter, Francesco, arrived with the liberating news that Cassino had fallen. The Allies were victorious and the monastery was destroyed down to its foundations.

Angelina didn't say a word. She disappeared and I didn't see her again until evening. All she said then was, "Who am I now referring to when I pray at Vespers, *'Destroy, oh God, the wicked'*?"

In the last week of May, we saw confusion all over the Latium plain. There were Germans withdrawing, hurrying northwards. Allies were following hot on their heels. And there were the refugees as well, with no idea where they were supposed to be heading. For several days we were worried the Germans might think of barricading themselves on our mountain where they could shoot down on the Via Casilana. But time did not allow.

We were without news for some time, as Francesco failed to come. All we knew was what we could see, and we were afraid for Rome because now that Cassino had fallen Rome was next in line.

But one evening Francesco re-appeared, out of breath and bursting with important news. The Germans had tried to negotiate with the Communists in Rome; they wanted to found an official Communist Republic.

We asked ourselves what this could mean. I simply couldn't believe it, but Angelina came up with an explanation. The Germans knew they couldn't stop the Allies marching into Rome, but the idea was this: the Rome they entered as conquerors would be nothing but a heap of rubble. The Germans didn't dare destroy Rome themselves. To have obliterated Rome would be a scandal that would last throughout history and never be expunged. But what if someone else undertook to do it? The task was to find someone who could be somehow provoked into doing it. It seemed a devilishly good plan. If Italy got a Communist Government there was bound to be a Revolution. In the massive confusion that would result, the Germans, either hiding behind the official ruling power or hindered by the necessity of guarding Rome against the Communists, could destroy Rome and push the blame onto the Communists. The Allies would find a ruined city, while the Communists would carry the stigma of an act of barbarism that could never be atoned for.

I couldn't believe any nation on earth would dare to destroy Rome, but Angelina said the Germans in their current state of desperation were capable of it, and it wouldn't be the first time Rome had been destroyed.

I've no idea whether the negotiations (which certainly did take place) truly sprang from such a malicious train of thought. But that evening we were beside ourselves with fear and indignation. I was in such a state that I said something I should never have said, although it was natural.

I said, "If only Antonio was with our people in Rome!"

It just slipped out. I didn't mean to cause Angelina pain, but I couldn't avoid seeing that I had.

Her voice sounded as though she were being strangled and couldn't breathe, but she spoke bravely in spite of it. "He will be in touch with them. If there is any way of making this plan fall through, Antonio will make sure it happens." It was the first time she had spoken his name again.

I summoned up hope and dared to say, "Shouldn't we be back with our own lot now? If my father knew I was sitting here in a convent peacefully hoe-ing garden beds..."

Angelina interrupted me.

"Instead of doing what? What would you want to do in Rome?"

"Be there!" I shouted.

"Then go," she said, quietly and simply.

"Yes, I will," I said. "And you? You're still able to stay? You don't feel driven to go?"

She shook her head. I challenged her then.

"That's because you're not Italian. It's not your country, not your Rome."

She looked at me with her eyes blazing. But then she calmed down and said simply. "That's what *you* think!"

She turned round and began to move away but had only gone three steps when she came

back and, without looking at me, asked this
question,

"Do you know what happened in Rome on
the 25th of March?"

How could I not know? What Italian
could ever forget that date and the numbers
involved: three hundred Italians for thirty
Germans. Thirty Germans had been killed
in a bomb attack on a German truck in the
Via Rasella. In return three hundred Italians
were shot in the Ardeatine caves.*

"That's when I *did* want to go back to Rome,"
she told me. "I wanted to starve with Rome, to
die with Rome if I had to. I took off this habit
and put on my old rags, packed my bundle
and was ready to go. This time I didn't slip or
sprain my foot. I left unhindered and didn't
once look round. But when I got as far as the
olive grove down there it suddenly occurred to
me that I had no pass, which meant I would
be arrested at the first control post, and what
then? I thought, I'll have to ask Francesco and
he'll get me his sister's pass or any sort he can,

Ardeatine caves: Site of the Ardeatine massacre. The victims
were transported to the Ardeatine caves in groups of five. They
were led into the caves with their hands tied behind their back
and then shot in the neck.

false or genuine. And I turned round and came back to wait for Francesco."

"And?" I queried. "Did you tell him and did he bring you a pass?"

"I did tell him but he didn't bring me one," she replied. "He was forbidden to come up on the mountain just then. You see it had gone warm and the people in the valley were talking of there being lots of dead bodies. The air was contaminated, they said, and the water polluted. The whole area was out of bounds."

I said stubbornly, "But he came back eventually. Did he have a pass with him?"

"He had forgotten it, and I left it at that, you understand."

"No, I don't. How can I? If it had been me, I should have gone without a pass," I said.

She didn't answer, and there was no need. I had understood. I believed in all sorts of 'signs' as well. But it irritated me that Angelina should believe in things I thought didn't match with her clear-thinking mind. I didn't want her to be like that — ordinary like the rest of us. I can see now, of course, that her simplicity was of a totally different kind, a kind that I now share, as do the rest of the nuns.

"Right," said Angelina. "You ought to be going now." She took a banknote out of the belt she always wore, folded it up small and pressed it into my hand.

The minute I had it in my hand I suddenly lost all desire to leave. I was ashamed. I looked about me at the walls eaten away by the destruction, the window arches, and the garden; I looked at Angelina and felt I couldn't go. But I was too proud to admit it. I gave her back the money.

"Hold on to it," I said. "I'll go tomorrow or the day after."

She didn't smile. After that there was no more talk of my going.

On the evening of the 3rd of June, Francesco arrived, hugging a large jar of wine and waving a loaf of bread like a victory flag.

He started shouting when he was still a long way off. Racing up the mountain almost choking — intoxicated with his news — he called out at least a dozen times, "Rome has fallen without any fighting!"

It transpired he was a day early (as we afterwards found out) but what did that matter? We celebrated the saving of Rome with Caprano wine and some of the German army's black bread, salvaged by Francesco from an overturned truck.

The war was over for Italians to the south of Rome.

⚜

A few days later the first of the townspeople who had fled from Maria del Monte came back full of joy at having survived — the possessions they had saved loaded on the backs of donkeys or in handcarts. Being alive seemed so much more important than coming back to nothing but bare walls, blackened beams and a few sooty copper pots lying in the rubble. People began to settle into what was left and to make all sorts of plans.

It didn't seem to occur to them that there was anyone alive in the convent. From the town side the convent looked like a complete ruin. The nuns had left when the rest did, so how could anyone be living there?

In the morning, however, our rooster gave us away. One of the two we kept had a penetrating voice and was in the habit of starting his crowing from the top of the walls. He would stand there for ages stretching up into the morning sky.

His call was the signal for Angelina to get up and say Lauds, and I generally got up at the same time to light the fire in the old stove and cook some porridge made of grated maize.

On that first morning after the inhabitants came back to Maria del Monte I heard a woman saying, "That's my rooster I left behind! Listen! Look, my rooster is still alive!" She coaxed him but he preferred to flutter back down into our garden.

That was when the first folk climbed over the walls. Keeping out of sight, I could see and hear what they said to each other when they discovered the carefully-tended garden, which they had never actually been in before because it was in the enclosure. They were quite aghast. They knew full well the nuns were still in Santa Agata, well hidden among various different households, and wearing civilian clothes. Whoever could have been doing the work here in the meantime?

And then Angelina arrived, wearing as always the black habit and — in completely unorthodox fashion — a white cloth like a headscarf the way a farmer's wife would do. Yet they at once perceived the nun in her. They flocked to her, kissing her hands and inundating her with questions. She wanted to get away from them, but how could anyone escape from a crowd of enthusiastic Italians without permission? Angelina did her best to explain that she wasn't a nun, but they didn't believe her because they didn't want to.

More and more clambered over the walls, and in the end she managed to get them to sit down. That done, she told them her story. But it only made them wonder at her all the more! They were quite overwhelmed with joy, and made her a present of the noisy rooster and all the hens — and the second rooster into the bargain.

The men started to examine the walls and some went straight off to fetch tools to make a cell for Angelina, and for me too.

"But I shan't stay here," Angelina told them. "Once your nuns come back I shall have to go."

It was the first time I had heard her say this. And the people cried out that they would have to see whether she would be allowed to leave, ever! Angelina said that what she *might* do would be to go away, finish her studies and come back as a doctor. I had never heard her say *that* before either. It seemed a very sensible idea to me.

An old woman, however, put her straight.

"You will never leave here. You're already wearing *this*," and she pointed to Angelina's habit.

"*This*?" exclaimed Angelina. "Why should this keep me here? I don't have to keep on wearing it."

"I tell you," replied the old woman stubbornly, "once you've put it on you'll *keep* it on, and that's it!"

"And what about her?" asked Angelina pointing at me. "Will she stay here, too?"

The old woman examined me carefully but only shrugged her shoulders, saying nothing.

Then they all left again to get on with their work.

"Are you *really* planning to do some more

studying," I asked Angelina, "and then come back here?"

"I don't know," she said quietly, "but perhaps I could."

***

It was now July, the height of summer. More and more people came back. It was obvious hardly anyone had stayed behind once the air raids had started. Most of them had got out in good time. Digging revealed only a few bodies covered in lime, and these were re-buried in the graveyard that lay far below the town where the ground was less rocky.

As far as the people of Santa Maria del Monte were concerned, the war was over. It's true they followed its future progress, but only half-heartedly.

They loved life, praised it, and were devoted to its service.

They hauled in mortar and repaired the water supply. They managed to get hold of an abandoned truck to use in bringing up building materials from the valley. And before long a market had opened up again in the piazza.

All of them were very poor but were overjoyed at finding themselves alive and back home.

***

In the evenings, they visited us in the convent and brought us the latest reports.

Through them we heard that Hitler had come within an inch of being killed in July; that the Allies were now advancing against Germany from the West, from France; and that it could only be a few months now until there was peace in Europe.

At the same time they were always begging Angelina for more details of her story, and they frequently persisted in asking me as well.

***

One day they arrived with the request that Angelina should read aloud to them and lead them in prayer in the evenings. You see, there was no priest in the place. Angelina was not happy with this notion. She found it a burden having the people around her.

They soon started coming to her about all sorts of things, not only hurt fingers and bits of dust in their eyes and once with a broken arm; they came with various moral dilemmas as well.

And one day a girl came asking to enter the convent, as if Angelina was in a position to decide on such a matter. That Angelina couldn't receive her was something she refused to accept, so she came every day to help us in the garden, and gradually prevailed upon Angelina to teach her the Benedictine Rule.

No one noticed how much Angelina suffered from being deprived of her solitude. But in the evenings she sighed often, and she rejoiced from the bottom of her heart when the day came for the convent to have its enclosure restored, and people could no longer slip over the walls or through the windows at any time of day or night.

But that time was long in coming.

Meanwhile the people began to rebuild part of the convent. Angelina had given them money. She told me the amount she had given them left only just enough for a ticket to Germany.

Strenuous work made the summer pass so quickly it seemed like a single long day. And suddenly, at the end of September, an English jeep drew up in front of the gateway that had now been cleared, and two nuns climbed out.

Obviously we ought to have realized the nuns would sooner or later come back, but Angelina went white with shock.

Before the nuns had even crossed the threshold she had disappeared, leaving me to receive them and explain things. I didn't want to either, and we were like children who think they have only to close their eyes to make what they're seeing vanish as if by magic.

It was no use. Soon a loud, pleasant-sounding voice was ringing along the convent corridor, "Angelina! Angelina! Giulia!"

I waited to see if Angelina would appear so that I could be next. She came, and I witnessed a scene that we had never expected, simply because we knew nothing about nuns and more especially nothing about our Mother Abbess.

Angelina walked forward slowly, shyly and very reluctantly. Her face was expressionless.

Mother Abbess stood quietly letting her approach. She looked at her with kindness and, when she was near enough, opened her arms to Angelina, who made no move in response. Instead, she said something I didn't grasp but, as she was pointing to her habit, I had to assume she was explaining how she had adopted it when it hadn't been given her.

The Abbess let her finish what she was saying, then she smiled and took the last few steps to where Angelina had found herself unable to go any further, and without more ado she put her arms around her.

I saw how Angelina resisted and squirmed, and then gave in. She even laid her head momentarily on the Abbess's shoulder. I could see her whole body relaxing and it wouldn't have surprised me if she had burst into tears. But she didn't.

The Abbess let go of her, and Angelina went on to take her and the younger nun (who was the cellaress at the time) to see the garden, and after that the convent.

It was not until they got as far as the corridor, that I finally dared to show myself!

The four of us then clambered about the

ruins eagerly examining things and making plans, as if the rebuilding of the convent concerned us all equally.

As was only to be expected, Mother Abbess finally got round to asking us if we wanted to stay.

I said, "No."

Angelina also said, "No," and added, "I'm going back to Germany when the war is over, to study."

"And till then?" asked the Abbess. "What are you going to do until the war *is* over?"

"Oh, I'm sure I'll find some sort of work somewhere or other," Angelina replied.

"And wouldn't you like to stay here for the time being?"

"No," repeated Angelina obstinately.

At that moment Mother Abbess stopped abruptly. Something had caught her attention, something that amused her. Following her gaze I saw it as well, and when she smiled, I smiled too. Angelina, you see, was standing directly beneath the old archway with its almost illegible inscription, '*egredere si potes.*'

She gave us a puzzled glance, but it was months before we told her why we had smiled.

"And you're absolutely sure you don't want to stay?" repeated the Abbess. "Not even if I beg you earnestly to help us? I'm short of people to do the work." She looked at Angelina with a twinkle in her eyes, already sure of victory.

"Very well then," Angelina said soberly. "I'll stay as long as I'm really needed."

Oh, Angelina, what a prophetic word you spoke at that moment! The day would *never* arrive when you were no longer needed in this convent!

Mother Abbess put the same question to me and I said I would see. I didn't know yet. What I *did* know was that I could never bear to be parted from Angelina.

After Mother Abbess and Sister Candida had gone away, everything then seemed different. We were only guests here now and they could ask us to leave. All the work we were doing was being done for others, for the rightful 'daughters' of this house.

But this was only one side of the change, the *dark* side. The other was much more remarkable. After the Abbess went, we felt a sense of loss. Something was missing. We couldn't wait for the day she came back.

We didn't share this openly, but after we had several times surprised each other climbing onto the wall at the sound of a vehicle coming up the mountain, we realized we were both waiting.

⚜

It is time I described our Mother Abbess, Sir, although you will get to know her anyway through reading the rest of my story. I'll just mention this much: she was sixty years old then, clever and energetic. She came from an old, noble family in Sienna, the Saracinis, who in times past were friends of the great Saint Catherine, the 'politician'.

Our Abbess is hard on herself and fasts so much that we wonder how she can keep healthy, but she discourages us from too much asceticism. She says she wants healthy, peaceful, sensible people in her convent.

She is temperamental and it must have cost her a great deal of effort to become the gentle, even-tempered and extremely loving person she is now. None of us has ever heard her say an unkind word. We all refer to her as

'La mamma'.

She and Angelina were especially drawn to each other from the first moment. But you will soon hear how strict she was in training your daughter.

❖

She came at last, at the end of October, in the old truck that belonged to the whole town and served as post-van, goods vehicle, bus and taxi. Twenty nuns arrived with her, those that were young, healthy and strong. The rest stayed in the little Priory of Santa Agata.

The nuns, all of them from somewhere between Rome and Naples, were lively, small-built and cheerful. And they gathered round us and drew us in as if we were not total strangers but rather long-lost children being welcomed home to the family. They were amazed at us and astounded at all we had done in the convent and garden.

Being Italian, I very soon felt close to them, although we in Umbria do not generally make friends quite as easily. But Angelina was shy and quiet, and soon she had to cope with her first hardship. The nuns had brought straw palliasses with them and blankets. They took over the two small rooms that had been rebuilt, those that are now parlors. They had to lie there like sardines in a tin. Angelina said some of them could come into our cells; there was plenty of room. But they said the Abbess had forbidden them to split up or sleep in the same room as us.

When we were alone again I told Angelina I found this a stupid arrangement, as we were all girls anyway and we couldn't pose any danger to the nuns if they were to sleep in the same room as us.

Angelina said grimly, "They're starting to keep their enclosure as far as they can. We're being shut out." I could feel how hurt she was, and started hoping again that she would soon give up wanting to live here.

That same evening she had another disappointment. For the first time, Compline was said in the choir again. We were allowed to be there but not to join in the singing. I didn't mind at all as I couldn't sing it anyway, but Angelina was very upset.

Another thing was that she no longer had

her breviary. She had left it lying in the chapel and one of the nuns had recognized it as hers and appropriated it. Angelina said nothing but she knelt bolt upright in the choir and stared stupidly in front of her without praying.

No one showed concern for her. It didn't seem to occur to anybody that it was *she* who had cleared choir and chapel of dust and dirt, and *she* who, all alone and glowing with fervor and devotion, had for many months kept up tradition by praying the Office.

At the end of Compline, when Mother Abbess started to intone Psalm 125 in celebration of the day, and everybody sang joyfully, '*When the Lord restored Sion, it seemed to us like a dream...Yes, great things has the Lord done for us, and we are glad*', Angelina crept out softly.

As electric light hadn't been reinstalled yet, everyone went straight to bed as soon as it got dark. I went into Angelina's cell and found her there, changing her clothes.

"Whatever are you doing?" I asked in alarm.

"You can see what I'm doing," she retorted. She had reached the end of her tether. She wanted to go.

"I'll go with you," I said.

She nodded. "I'll be waiting for you in the garden but not until an hour after the Abbess has blown her candle out."

I expected to feel happy the minute I had at last made a sensible decision, after all these months full of pious dreams. But I didn't. I had no idea why. However, I suppressed my strange ache and packed my bundle.

I then waited until it was dark enough for me to creep through the corridor unseen. But when I reached the garden I noticed there was still a light in the Mother Abbess's cell. I stayed where I was, not making a sound. I sat down on a stone and waited. Angelina was not there yet.

It was a beautiful night and still warm. The hundreds of crickets in the pines and olive trees were making their music. Strong scents were wafting from herbs and flowers, all grown by Angelina and me in the garden. And one of our roosters crowed once sleepily, dreaming maybe.

All this made me realize how much this place had become a part of me. Yet I was still set on leaving, and without delay.

At last I heard very light footsteps

approaching. "Angelina," I whispered. But it was not Angelina, it was the Mother Abbess.

"Child," she said, "what are you doing out here? You'll catch cold. Come in." I had no choice but to stand up and obey.

Then she put her hand on my shoulder and said, "It's no good waiting for Angelina. She's going to stay here."

"No!" I cried. "She's *not* going to stay. We're leaving — *both* of us, *tonight!*"

"Come with me," she said, and led me to Angelina's door which stood ajar. I heard Angelina breathing deeply and peacefully. She was asleep.

"What have you done to her?" I whispered.

"Now you go and sleep, too," she said quietly. She made the sign of the cross on my forehead and I went obediently to bed, a stranger to myself.

***

The next morning Angelina, transformed and happy, told me all about it. As she had crept past the Mother Abbess's cell, the door had opened and she had heard Mother's gentle voice saying simply, *"Figlia mia,** where are you going?"* In some mysterious way these words had taken hold of her and, without really understanding why, she had flung herself into Mother's arms.

This had made her drop her bundle. The Abbess had picked it up and taken it back to Angelina's cell. She had put her to bed, giving her the night blessing as a mother would her child, and Angelina had sunk at once into a deep, sound sleep.

"And what now?" I asked. "Are you really going to stay?"

"Yes, I think so," she said. "How about you?"

"No, I'm not," I said. "But I'll still be here to help."

Work started the following day. Laborers arrived with a big digger and began to clear away the rubble. Trucks brought lime, roof-tiles and wooden beams for rafters, and it all arrived at the same time, although it must have cost a fearful amount.

**Figlia mia:* My daughter.

Where did all these things come from? And who provided the money to pay for them? I asked the sisters but they had no idea and were not concerned because they were used to everything turning up at their convent as and when needed. The Sister Cellaress quoted these words, "*Cum dederit dilectis suis somnum*'. 'The Lord gives to his chosen ones while they sleep'."

That's the way it was and still is today. We are a poor convent and there are days when we haven't one lira left to spend. But Mother Abbess always says, "We'll be getting something tomorrow."

The first time I heard her say it I asked where from.

"I don't know yet, my children, but I do know we shall be getting something." And so we did.

After a while I stopped asking or being surprised, and learned to wait and trust as the others did.

However, one day towards the end of November we ran out of money and had no more building materials. We were worried, and I began thinking the work would be left unfinished; also that our method of waiting and trusting without anxiety would have to be radically revised. I was almost glad. (Why should a convent be set apart from the massive workings of the world's economy?)

The next morning Mother Abbess announced she was going to drive to Rome and visit the Allied Command, and that she wanted me with her as interpreter. There was great alarm in the convent because everyone was afraid of the English and the Americans. And no one had the slightest idea how we were going to get to Rome.

But exactly one hour later our *Baumeister**
drove in from Frosinone and took us back with him. From there we got a truck belonging to the Allies, and by midday were actually in Rome. Finally we found ourselves standing in front of an officer, who half-listened to our

---

*Baumeister: The man in charge of the construction work.

request and then told us unkindly that he had more important things to see to, and what's more he was Anglican.

"Sorry to have bothered you," Mother Abbess gave him her loveliest smile. But she didn't go. Instead she simply stood her ground and fixed the officer with her gaze. She looked at him in such a way that he felt forced to ask what more we wanted, and did we think he was Head of the Bank of England and could give us a loan.

"A loan?" cried Mother Abbess. "We don't want to borrow anything, we're asking for a gift."

The officer was rather put out by this, but just then another man came in, and he was a superior officer. It was explained to him what we were there for, and he laughed. He took us with him and let us tell him all about it, after which he laughed still more but finished up promising that he would help us, and that we could go back home without any worries.

We did, without staying a minute longer in Rome. We got a lift with an Italian van that picked us up right at the start of the Via Casilina.

The conversation at the Command had

infuriated me because I couldn't believe the officer would keep his promise. I confided in Mother Abbess but she was in the best possible mood, quite sure she had achieved what she had set out to do.

And she was right, of course. The very next day the officer came from Rome in a jeep and surveyed everything we had built. (At that stage very little of it was within the enclosure, where he was not allowed to go. Everything else was still open.) Next he asked for a list of everything we still needed. Finally, leaving us a box of conserves and a bundle of banknotes, he next drove off to our *Baumeister* to get more precise details.

A few days later, trucks arrived bringing boards, lime, cement, stone flags, oil-based paint, and wood-stains; and it was all paid for. We looked on it as a miracle.

The officer came back more than once. He informed us he belonged to the family of the great Archbishop Newman of Canterbury,* but he laughed when he said it and we were never sure when he was being serious and when he was teasing.

---

*Archbishop Newman was never Archbishop of Canterbury!

There was one occasion when we were sure he meant what he said. In May 1945, when he came for the last time because he had been ordered back to England, he told us he was delighted to have got to know our Abbess and "this hallowed place", as he called our convent.

The building was finished just in time for Christmas, and we had all the essential furnishings. What's more we had a priest now, living in the presbytery that had been built on to the convent.

The day before the Feast, the last few nuns came home from the Priory. At Christmas the Bishop was to re-consecrate the convent and church, and the convent would regain its strict enclosure. This also meant the day had arrived when Angelina and I would no longer be allowed to live within the enclosure unless we belonged to the convent.

I had already made up my mind. I wouldn't enter* but I wanted to stay till the end of the war, working and living in the presbytery.

---

*Enter: join the Benedictine Order as a novice

I didn't know what Angelina was going to do. I was hoping with all my heart she would join me in my decision. Her plan of going back to Germany and picking up on her studies in medicine was so sensible and good.

I wanted to talk to her about it but when I tried she just said, "Please, be quiet!" and left me standing. I didn't see her again all day.

That evening she came looking for me between supper and Compline, and she seemed to be in a great hurry. "Come on," she said. "It's high time we said goodbye to Mother Abbess, and tomorrow morning early we'll be on our way."

"Early tomorrow?" I gasped. "Why? I'd rather stay until the war is over."

"Come *on*!" she repeated urgently.

"Good," I said. "Then I can ask her at the same time about whether I can live in the presbytery."

Angelina didn't answer. Instead she took hold of my arm and quickly steered me into the Abbess's room, as if there not a second to lose.

Mother received us with kindness as she always did.

"You talk first," Angelina told me, and I put my request.

Mother said another possibility would be for me stay in the convent, in a guest room outside the enclosure. Then she looked at Angelina. "Now," she said. "Haven't you got your little bundle with you?"

Then I heard Angelina say, *"Ehrwürdige Mutter,** I wish to apply to enter your order."

There was silence for a while. Angelina had turned white.

I don't know what I had expected but it was certainly not the completely serious question Mother put to her. "And your studies? You cannot study medicine as a Benedictine."

To my astonishment I heard Angelina answer very quietly, "I shall be content to be directed to some other kind of work here."

The Abbess took this in without any sign of surprise. Then she opened a book lying on the table and read aloud from it:

"'Hard and rough is the way that leads to God. You must renounce your own will entirely; you must daily do the will of those who are your superiors, who from time to

---

**Ehrwürdige Mutter*: Literally 'Honorable Mother'.

time will lay on you heavy and troublesome burdens to test your patience, your obedience and your humility.'"

When she had finished reading, she looked at Angelina for a long while and Angelina returned her gaze calmly and openly.

Then the Abbess took another small book, the shape of which was already familiar to me from seeing it often in Angelina's hands. It was the 'Rule' and slowly she read, "'The abbot shall make no distinction between persons in the abbey. He shall not love one more than another.'"

She stopped and again looked at Angelina. This time Angelina looked down, but Mother kept on looking at her until Angelina looked up again.

Then she leafed through the breviary and read:

The Lord will free the people of Israel, free them from the hands of the mighty. They shall come home singing songs, and hasten rejoicing to the table of the Lord's gifts. There shall be corn and wine and oil. They shall hunger no more.

It took me a while to work out why she had chosen this particular passage, and even Angelina needed to ponder it. Before she had even begun to take it in the Abbess began a series of questions which hit *me* hard, and must therefore have struck Angelina like a hammer blow. She spared her nothing. And she suddenly dropped the familiar form of 'you'.

"Are you prepared," she said, speaking formally, "from this day on to have absolute trust in God to provide you with a just portion of this world's goods? Will you cast out from mind and heart any political concerns? Are you sure you will not one day accuse yourself of fleeing from the battle? Are you aware that from now on you will have no means of helping to change the world apart from your prayer and your sacrifice? Will this kind of participation in the fate of your fellow human beings satisfy you?"

And then she added what seemed to me a terrible question: "Are you quite sure you don't want to live side by side with your Antonio, and work together in politics?"

Angelina had first turned her head away

slightly, like someone trying to evade a painful blow, but now she turned to face the Abbess frankly and with courage.

"*Ehrwürdige Mutter,*" she answered, "I trust a year in the novitiate will help make this clear to me."

"Good," replied the Superior. "Go now. We'll have another talk tomorrow."

As Angelina moved towards the door she swayed and I was afraid she would faint, but before I could reach her, Mother was there with her arms round her.

I went out and left the two of them alone.

I waited in the corridor.

When Angelina finally re-appeared, but passed me without seeing me, I went back into the Superior's room.

"I want to join your order, too," I said.

She smiled.

"Yes," she said, stroking my hair lovingly. "You, too. Together we will give it a try."

We both entered the novitiate on the 10th of February — the Feast Day of Saint Scholastica, Saint Benedict's sister.

Four months later, and a few weeks after the end of the war, Angelina was summoned to see the Mother Abbess. She was so pale when she came out that we all crowded round her, asking if she was ill or if something terrible had happened. She pushed us away, gently and silently, and hurried into the chapel. I waited for her – for a long time.

When she came out at last, she whispered, "Antonio's here. He's in the parlor." Then she went down, slowly and calmly.

***

It was several years before Angelina told me what happened at that meeting. Mother had said that Antonio had arrived and had spoken with her, asking if Angelina was still free and able to leave with him. He wanted to marry her. Mother had told him Angelina was still free and he could ask her himself. She told Angelina she would offer no advice but remarked that Antonio was good, clever and brave, and a man who had a great and powerful love for her; that he had an important position in the new government and could change things for the better; and that it would be no bad decision should she wish to spend her life with him.

Angelina was furious. "Whatever have I done to make you not want to keep me?"

Unperturbed, Mother answered, "You misunderstand me. I neither want to keep you nor send you away. You have to decide. Married life is also good and ordained by God."

"Why are you tempting me like this?" asked Angelina.

"Go now," the Abbess said.

Angelina was near to tears. "Please, spare me this task."

But Mother answered severely, "Go. Running away will not solve anything. Face this meeting. God will help you."

And Angelina went.

As you have seen, Sir, our parlor has a double grille and there is no way of holding hands. Also, unless you get very close, you can only see each other dimly.

Angelina told me Antonio was walking up and down with a very bad limp (having been badly wounded), and had a stick the sound of which on the stone-flagged floor was almost unbearable. She had crept up to the grille and it was a long time before he noticed her. She saw him, however, and she didn't need to tell me what she felt.

Then she started to speak. She asked him where he was living and about his work. She asked him about the progress of the reforms she had heard of. And he answered her politely and soberly.

The Communist Party was powerful, in a position of leadership; many large estates had been divided up; settlements for workers were planned; the war had therefore been worthwhile and a better time had begun.

Then they were both silent.

Antonio stopped walking to and fro but did not come up to the grille. He stayed in the middle of the room and from there he asked the question he had come to ask.

"And you, Angelina? Will you come with me

now as my wife? You know there's never been any other woman in my life apart from you, and there never will be."

But all she said was, "You know yourself it is not meant to be. Why did you come?"

He answered quietly.

"Right!" he said, hurt. "Why *did* I come?" Then he moved to the grille with one stride and cried out, "Why? Why? If you don't know..."

"Please forgive me," Angelina interrupted, "but I cannot come with you. I have made up my mind. This is final. Forget me, or better still renounce me..."

She had no strength for more. She told me they looked at each other through the dark, double grille and then Antonio went out quickly and was gone forever.

***

More than three years went by before Angelina was ready to tell me all this, but even this length of time had not been enough to blot out the memory of Antonio.

"You must have loved him so much!" I said.

"Yes," she replied simply. "I did love him, and I still do in my own way. I always will. But the love and the pain...what are they compared to the '*dove*' that has '*escaped from the snare of the fowler*' and '*found her nest*'?* You know the answer yourself. And now let's not talk about it ever again."

And that, Sir, is the end of my story.

You know all about Antonio's progress. His name is daily in the papers.

You also know that Angelina's path is not smooth, yet she is happy in spite of it and much loved by everyone. All that remains is for me to implore you to let your love for your daughter extend to loving her destiny also, and the One who ordained it, both for her and for you.

---

*Passages from the Psalms that speak of freedom of spirit.

About the Author

Luise Rinser was born April 1911 in Pitzling, Upper Bavaria and was educated in a *Volksschule* in Munich, scoring high marks in her exams. She refused to join the Nazi Party but did belong to its Women's Association from 1936, and also to the Teachers' Association.

Like the heroine of *Leave If You Can*, its author was never afraid to step out.

In teaching and writing, she followed the reformer Franz Seitz. Then, during World War II, she risked her life. In 1939 she had given up teaching to marry the composer Hörst Gunther Schnell, by whom she had two sons. However he died on the Russian Front, and in 1944 she was denounced for undermining military morale and imprisoned at Traunstein. Only the end of the war saved her from the death sentence. Her *Prison Diary* was the first book to be published in Germany after the war (1946).

Rinser was active in the political and social discussions in post-war Germany. From 1945 to 1953, she lived in Munich and was a freelance writer for the *New Daily News*.

She was familiar with communist ideals, and though profoundly misled about certain religious and moral issues, she remained a Catholic throughout her life. She was an accredited journalist at the Second Vatican Council.

By the time *Leave If You Can* came out in 1959, Rinser already had six full-length novels and several short stories to her credit. Over the next forty years she wrote novels, autobiographical works, books for children and teens, and special writings of a political, social and philosophical nature. Throughout her life Rinser was a respected writer and thinker in secular circles and won many awards in literary and other fields.

She lived for a while in Rome and later near to Rome, and in the course of her work travelled to many countries including the United States and Japan.

She survived into the twenty-first century, and died in Munich in 2002.

If you enjoyed this book, you might also be interested in these other high-quality works from Arx Publishing...

Angels in Iron by Nicholas C. Prata
"The novel's principal strength is its attention to historical detail and the unrelenting realism with which the battle scenes—and there are many—are described....In addition to being an exciting action/adventure yarn and quite a page-turner, *Angels in Iron* is valuable as a miniature history lesson....This is a book that belongs on the bookshelf of every Catholic man, should be read by every Catholic boy (11 or older, I would say), and stocked by every Catholic school library."
—*Latin Mass Magazine*

Belisarius: The First Shall Be Last by Paolo A. Belzoni
"The book strikes one as a conservative rallying cry to the "Christian West" today....It presents and argues for, in an understated way, a Christian way of war, to be waged by manly men who value purity and patriotism for the sake of preserving Christian civilization. An ambitious tale, filled with action, spectacle, and intrigues of all kinds....Painstakingly authentic in its historical, military, and religious detail, assiduously researched and replete with facts."
—John J. Desjarlais, *CatholicFiction.net*

Niamh and the Hermit by Emily C. A. Snyder
"When I first saw this book, I feared that it might be just another effort to hook on to the Tolkien wagon. It is not. Very far from that. It is wholly original, and all I can say is that it is beautiful, beautiful, beautiful. The author is entirely in control of her narrative, and, drawing on the tradition of ancient Celtic tales, gives us something genuinely new. What we have here is a very noble achievement."
—Thomas Howard, author of *C. S. Lewis: Man of Letters*

Crown of the World: Knight of the Temple by Nathan Sadasivan
"*Knight of the Temple* is written in a style of historical fiction that was prevalent in American Catholic literature several decades ago and follows in the footsteps of such Catholic classics as *The Outlaws of Ravenhurst* and the novels of Louis de Wohl, but with greater intensity. *Knight of the Temple* is a really excellent work, fraught with tension, that hooks us for part two."
—Phillip D. Campbell III, *Saint Austin Review*

The Laviniad: An Epic Poem by Claudio R. Salvucci
"The author successfully writes in the style of the ancient epic in modern English. Lovers of classic tales will really appreciate the poetry and the plot. The poem reads easily and naturally with the flow and flavor of the ancient epics."
—*Favorite Resources for Catholic Homeschoolers*

For further information on these titles, or to order, visit:
www.arxpub.com

CPSIA information can be obtained at www.ICGtesting.com
Printed in the USA
BVOW071526090812

297475BV00001B/4/P